NOTHING FORBIDDEN

KENNY WRIGHT

KW PUBLISHING
WWW.KENNYWRITER.COM

NOTHING FORBIDDEN

PROLOGUE

"Another cocktail?" the bartender asked Katie. He was attractive in a hard, macho way—dark hair formed into a faux hawk, an earring, a deep tan. The kind of guy she shouldn't go for, but did.

"Um, I shouldn't..."

The bartender had a broad nose that looked like it had been broken a time or two. It suited him. "You never do things that you shouldn't?"

The question sent a shiver through her. "Most of the time, yes," she said. "But I'll take another punch."

"Coming right up."

Her stomach fluttered at his smile.

Katie had been like this more and more since her husband had filled her head with his fantasy. He wanted her to have sex with other men? Every time she thought about it, it left her confused all over again. They'd been together forever, and she wanted to support him, whatever his fantasy was. But hearing him admit to these things was like waking up next to a stranger. Where had it come from? Why had he never said something like that before?

Coming to The James after their meetings today felt right. The trendy speakeasy was on the same block as their hotel, was quiet enough to have a pop-up meeting, as her colleagues called it, and the drinks were great. That was one of the problems—they were so great, she'd had too many.

Katie watched the bartender mix her drink, his back to her. He filled out his black shirt well, broad shoulders and thick arms hinting at a toned body beneath. Not too muscular—she always liked soccer player bodies over the weightlifting type, and this guy fit the bill.

She shook her head. *Fit the bill?* "This is your fault, Max," she muttered as the bartender returned with a glass blossoming with fruit.

"What's that?" he said.

"Nothing. Just thinking that I really shouldn't have ordered another."

"Big day tomorrow? Or was today your big presentation?" he said.

"How do you know that's why I'm here?"

"Well, you're not here to meet anyone. You came in with co-workers. And you talked mostly business. You're still in your suit..."

Katie took mental inventory of herself. It was true; she was still in her dark skirt suit, her auburn hair still pinned back and professional. She wasn't one to rely on her femininity to win contracts and make successful presentations, but as this guy checked her out, she became self-conscious of how snug the black pencil skirt was, or how the black blouse hinted at her pale, freckled cleavage.

The bartender's eyes drifted there now and she wished she'd buttoned the blouse up to her neck. "Nice suit, by the way."

"Thanks." Katie blushed. "My presentation was today. Tomorrow, we talk details."

"The fun stuff." He pointed at the punch. "You definitely need that. Consider it on me."

He had a confidence that reminded Katie of her husband when they'd first met—a bartender in his twenties, just like this young man. "Trying to get me drunk to take advantage of me?" she asked.

He leaned on the bar across from her. "Do you want to be taken advantage of?"

Katie met his eyes, dark and unwavering, and felt part of herself melt. She plucked a pineapple wedge from the glass of punch and bit into the sweet fruit. She could have this guy as easily as she could that pineapple. All she had to reach out and take.

Not that she had any intention of going there. Max's fantasy was crazy, and it was messing with her head. Still, it was fun to flirt.

"You're pretty successful with women, I bet," she said.

The guy pulled back, giving her space, but didn't seem fazed or rejected. So much confidence in youth. "I do alright."

"You have a girlfriend?"

"A few."

Katie laughed. "Of course you do. And what would they think if they saw you hitting on me?"

"They're not here. Why does it matter?"

Of course he'd say that, too, she thought. "It matters." She held up her ring. "One day, it'll matter."

"And yet here you are, talking to me. Having a drink...flirting with *me.*"

"I don't even know your name."

"But that makes it even more fun, doesn't it? Look around you. You don't know anyone, and they don't know you. You can be anyone you want to be."

"What makes you think I'm unhappy being who I am right now?"

"Which is?"

A happily married woman and a mom, she thought. It felt like the right thing to think, and probably the right thing to say. Instead, she said, "Someone who's about to settle my tab, go back to my room next door, and have a fitful night's rest."

The guy nodded. "Would it make a difference if I told you that today was my birthday, and you'd be the perfect present?"

They both laughed at the cheese in the line.

"You'd do better off asking me for a map *because you got lost in my eyes,*" she said.

"Green eyes always do get me all turned around," he said with a grin.

God, why did he have to be so charming?

She batted her lashes. "Sorry about that, but I'm still going to call it a night." As she looked up at him, she was glad she had the bar between them. The barrier put her at ease, despite those dark, butterfly-inducing eyes.

"But what about that drink? You're not going to let it go to waste, are you?"

"Of course not," she said. Picking up the drink, she downed it all in one mighty gulp, then stood. "Thanks for the punch." She brushed her hair over her ears, then immediately regretted it. It was a childish gesture she'd tried to teach herself to stop doing, but would sneak in when she was drunk...or talking to guys like this one.

"Thanks for the company."

"Goodnight," she said. Turning, she was surprised to see she was one of the only people in the place. What time was it?

****

Outside felt better—an October evening in the city. Katie wasn't a huge fan of the bustle of New York, but she couldn't deny the electricity that permeated it. The entrance to The James was tucked away in an alley, as a speakeasy should be. Even here, off the main drag, she felt the energy fizz and pop around her.

Or maybe that buzz had more to do with the drinks than the city. She felt ten years younger, untethered from the trappings of adulthood. For the briefest of moments, all the things that defined her fell away: her job, her husband, her daughter. She was free.

But free to what? Certainly not free to actually pursue a man like that bartender. For the first time since Max had mentioned his desire for her to be with other men, Katie realized that she could make it happen. Not that she would, but she *could*.

Her adrenaline spiked—guilt coming right along with it. She shouldn't even be entertaining these thoughts, no matter what her husband thought that he wanted. It was wrong. It wasn't normal. She'd pledged to spend the rest of her life with Max, and part of that meant being only with *him*...

Yet even as she reminded herself of what was proper, she couldn't stop thinking about the bartender—about his faux hawk, the thick cords of his forearms, and the promise of more beneath his shirt. He was strange. New. Exciting. She didn't do his laundry. She hadn't had to figure out how to change diapers with him.

And when he'd looked at her, he saw a sexy woman in a business suit, not Mrs. Max Callahan, daughter of a prominent Connecticut family. He saw a woman he wanted to dominate.

"This is all your fault, Max," she said again. She reached the doors to her hotel.

"Evening," the doorman said.

Katie felt his eyes linger on her ass as she walked through the lobby.

She looked at the world through the lens of an accountant—it had always been that way, even before she attained her CPA license. She saw this fantasy in terms of debt and payment. Had she gone back to her room with the bartender, or the doorman, or the cute concierge who'd initially suggested The James, she'd be accruing debt.

The question was: what was Max expecting as payment? He couldn't just want an account of it. That didn't balance for her. Did he want to sleep with another woman? That was the obvious answer, although he'd already denied it. Maybe something had happened already and this was some form of repayment.

Her body went cold. Her scalp lit up, fiery with jealousy. She knew it was impossible, but her head went there anyway, the night's booze ushering it along. Max was good-looking. She'd been attracted to him from the time she'd first met him at sixteen, but back then, all she saw was his smile and a guy who wanted to hook up with her. And back then, as now, she thought of herself as above that.

Katie fought to get her head on straight. She was all over the place. She focused on getting to her room first. The elevator buttons seemed fuzzier than they should have been, and she had trouble remembering which floor she was on.

It was only when she finally got up to her room that she realized that her purse was missing.

Panic set in, wild and uncaged. Even with the light buzz, her analytical brain started working through the problem. Last place she used it: The James. Closing her tab. Which meant one more meeting with that bartender. Her chest tightened. Her body buzzed, all the way out to her fingertips.

Once upon a time, she'd been dared to steal a pair of sunglasses from the mall. She could have afforded them, of course. That wasn't the point. The point was to do something bad. Something completely against her nature.

Back then, walking into the department store, she'd been jittery with excitement. She felt exactly the same way returning to The James. Suddenly, the alley leading toward it felt more dangerous. Reaching for the doorbell felt so much more clandestine.

When the bartender himself opened the door before she could ring it, she practically fell backwards. He caught her, pulling her against him. He felt like stone beneath his shirt—warm, breathing stone.

"Sorry about that. Didn't see you there," he said. Then he released her.

"I...I forgot my purse," Katie sputtered.

He held up what appeared to be her purse. "And I've got it. Was bringing it over to your hotel, actually."

She knew he probably meant the front desk, but thoughts of this guy knocking on her door as she got ready for bed sent a jolt through her.

"Thanks. Such a gentleman."

The guy grinned and Katie's knees weakened. "How about a reward for my good deed?"

"But I ended up coming back for it."

"You still don't have it," he pointed out. When she reached to take it from him, he pulled it back and away.

"Really?" She reached again, but he held it higher. Losing her balance, she caught herself on his hard chest. She could feel the heat rise off his body through his shirt, could smell the cologne he wore, and the musk of sweat and masculinity beneath that.

Turning to look up at him, she realized that he was right there, his lips just inches away.

The moment slowed down, each action experienced in hyper reality. He wrapped an arm around her waist. He pulled her against him, trapping her hand between them. She could feel his excitement against her hip. Could feel his heart thud beneath her fingertips.

There was plenty of time to escape. To push him away. To turn her head. To say *no*.

Instead, Katie let the inevitable happen. The hand on her waist tightened, pulling her even closer. His other hand found the back of her neck, pulling her head up to his—her lips up to his.

The kiss was fiery. Illicit. So wrong, yet so incredibly good. He pushed his tongue into her mouth and she did nothing to stop him. She let him. She welcomed him with her own tongue.

It was only when she felt his hand drift across her ass that she came to her senses. Pulling back, she said, "We can't."

"Sure we can."

"We shouldn't."

"Tell me you don't want it."

She tried to form the words, but couldn't. She was too dazed, too caught up in the moment. He stepped into her again, taking hold of her and spinning her around until she was up against the brick wall of the alley. He pinned her there, arms on either side of her, mouth once again descending. She let him kiss her again. Let him kiss along her jaw and into the crook of her neck.

She could feel his breath against her ear as he leaned in to whisper. "Tell me you don't want to fuck me, and I'll stop."

Her pussy tingled.

When his lips found hers again, she kissed him like she didn't want him to stop. Maybe, for a split second, she didn't. She kissed him back, hard, her fingers lacing through his hair, tussling the product-perfect set of it. She pulled him close, let herself be smothered in his strangeness. His newness.

Then she pushed him away.

She was out of breath, but managed to find her voice. "I'm not going to fuck you."

"But you want to."

Katie smiled, feeling control return with her senses. "Maybe. But I'm not going to."

The guy nodded, hands up. "Fair enough."

Katie plucked her purse from his hand. "Have a good night, birthday boy. You're going to have to settle on a kiss as your present."

He smiled. "Your loss…"

Your loss… His words followed her back to her hotel room, mixed in with her own giddy thoughts. Did that really just happen? Did she just kiss another man—some stranger whose name she didn't even know? Again, she thought about her one shoplifting experience, and the rush of adrenaline that she'd felt walking out of there with the sunglasses in her purse. She could barely breathe then, just as she could barely breathe now.

Back in her hotel room, she slipped naked beneath the rich Egyptian cotton bed sheets, stared out at the New York skyline, and found her pussy waiting for her touch.

CHAPTER 1

One year later...

Katie buried her face in the pillow, her moans more growls than cries. She raised her ass higher, changing the angle of the cock pounding her from behind. So good. So full...

She turned her head enough to breathe, her red hair spilling across her face, sticky with sweat.

"Tell me more, Katie. Tell me more," her husband said behind her.

"I loved how he kissed me. How he pushed me up against the wall and took me."

Her mind was back in New York a year ago, when the lifestyle they now led was just a fantasy. Even though it had been just a kiss, it had been a defining moment for her. It was only then that she realized that this fantasy was as much hers as it was Max's—it just took her the next few months to accept.

On her knees, ass high, head low, she reached between her legs, fingers following the narrow strip of trimmed curls to her clit. She could feel Max's cock slide in and out of her—feel the perfect fit of him, familiar yet ever sexy. She worked her clit in time with his thrusts, flicking the swollen button as she raced to orgasm.

"Did you feel his cock when he kissed you?" Max demanded.

"Yes!" She had. And he was big and hard. "He felt so good."

"And you were tempted to take him back up to your room?"

"Yes, baby. I was *so* tempted. I wanted him to tear my clothes off and take me." Katie moaned as Max's thrusts sped up. She knew exactly how to press his buttons, and after a year in their more open lifestyle, she pressed them without hesitation. "If he had brought my purse to my hotel room...if he'd kissed me in the privacy of my own room...I don't think I could have stopped him..."

Max grunted, his hips slapping wetly with each penetration. Katie shut her eyes, and suddenly it was the bartender behind her—the bartender lodged inside her. She imagined how hot he must be naked: a muscled upper body, six pack, a thick cock that he knew how to use...

"Fuck me, baby! Har—der!"

To the young bartender, she'd be just another notch on his bedpost. She'd be one of a long string of conquests. The idea should have disgusted her—it did...mostly. The feminist in her gnashed and roared. The successful accountant in her objected to the imbalanced books.

But a sliver of her was turned on by the prospect—the same sliver who'd had a one-night stand back in college, or liked muscles and a cocky attitude, or who still thought back to her experiences with Chloe and Greg with lust, despite all that had happened.

"You're thinking about him, aren't you?" Max asked.

"Uh...yes."

"Keep thinking of him. Keep thinking...of him!"

Max grabbed her ass, squeezing hard enough that it hurt, and exploded inside her. The liquid heat ignited her own orgasm, which surged forth. She buried her face in her pillow and stifled her cries as best she could. It was late, Mya's room was down the hall, but Katie watched herself out of habit.

They clung to each other, enjoying the glow of their shared climax. She shuddered as Max continued to pulse inside her, even when he had nothing left to give. She loved the aftershocks.

She loved this man.

****

"I can't believe it's been a year since that kiss," Max said to the ceiling. They were beneath the sheets, although Katie lay with her breasts bared, still overheated from the sex. "So much has happened..."

Katie snuggled up to Max, draping her leg over him. Her hand casually drifted down to his cock, soft and wet. "You mean you opening a new bar? Or that we've had sex with two other couples?"

In any other situation, she'd never be so cavalier about sex, but something about this lifestyle—and the way it affected her husband—empowered her to be bold. She felt his cock stir in his hand.

"And how about you exploring your bi side?" he asked.

The emotions that that stirred were complex. She still found it hard to believe that she'd had sex with another woman—it was thrilling and deviant and frightening all at once. Katie still didn't consider herself "bisexual," despite the two separate girl-on-girl experiences, and the idea of it was in direct competition with the tightly controlled woman she considered herself to be.

But she couldn't deny being turned on by those encounters,

both at the time and now, thinking about it. Max loved it too, and she had just as much fun bringing it up as he did.

"How about *you* watching me get taken by another man as I go down on another woman?" she asked.

Max's cock grew thick enough that she could stroke it. "That's so sexy," he said.

Katie pumped his shaft. They kissed one another, slow and languid, while all the while she stroked his ever-growing erection.

When they parted, Max said, "You could have slept with him, you know."

"Who?"

"The birthday boy."

"I know that now. I didn't then."

Max nodded, giving her a funny look. She knew that look. He wanted to say something, but didn't. That look always got them in trouble.

"Spit it out, Max."

"It would've been pretty hot if you'd have gone for it." He traced his fingers along the contours of her full breasts. "Greg told me once that the hottest encounters that Chloe had were the ones he *didn't* know about."

Katie knew a little about that. Arguably the architect of their new lifestyle, Chloe Reynolds and her husband had seduced Katie into bed, then had done everything they could to destroy her marriage. They'd almost succeeded when Chloe nearly convinced Max that Katie was having an affair during a business trip to Hong Kong—something she absolutely did not do. In the end, Max and Katie emerged stronger because of it, but the damage to their trust in others lingered still. They hadn't played since the opening of The Katherine, when emotions had overflowed and they'd fallen into bed with their friends, Nadia and John.

When she didn't respond immediately, Max read the wrong thing into it. "Chloe also said that you were *particularly interested in those affairs*. Something like that..."

Katie felt Max's cock stiffen in her hand. Is that what he wanted? She hoped not, because she wasn't about to give it to him.

"Chloe is a bad person," Katie said, unable to keep the anger from her voice. "You can't trust anything she said. Do I need to remind you that she nearly ruined our marriage?"

"No, no. Of course not. And I know she's a terrible human being. Greg, too. But..." Again, he hesitated. This time, Katie tried finishing the thought.

"But part of you is turned on by what a slut she was."

"I guess," he said.

This is the part of the fantasy that Katie always got hung up on. Did Max want her to be like Chloe? To fuck around? To be a self-centered whore? Because she couldn't do that—had no desire to.

"Why? Do you realize that she had no respect for her husband? She told me as much. She told me that she had the life: she could fuck around with whoever, whenever, without limit, and could go home to her millionaire husband, who'd support her no matter what. She's awful."

Thankfully, none of her words registered as a pulse along Max's cock.

"I know. And I don't want you to be like that." He hugged her against him, kissing her lips gently. "I don't want you to be someone you're not. But over the last year, I've seen a new you emerge, and you have no idea how sexy that woman is."

Katie squeezed him. "Oh, I have some idea."

Max brightened. "I just want you to know that I trust you." He

NOTHING FORBIDDEN   15

hesitated before adding, "And between us, there are no limits."

She screwed up her face. "Chloe and Greg aren't off limits?"

"Would you really jump back into bed with them if they offered?"

"Of course not." She wrinkled her face in disgust.

"And I know that. I trust your judgment. So yes, no limits. If you're having fun, then so am I."

She processed it, but still didn't fully understand it. "So if I told you that I really did invite the bartender back to my room a year ago—and that I've been seeing him every time I go back to visit—"

She stopped when she felt his cock stiffen. Looking up at him, eyes wide, she said, "Really?"

He licked his lips, a man uncertain of what he wanted. "You didn't actually do that, did you?"

Katie felt the flash of frustration blaze through her. After all that they'd been through—after Greg and Chloe and Hong Kong— why wasn't he furious at even the suggestion that she had an affair?

She couldn't deny that instead, it turned him on. She had proof in hand. Swinging her leg over his body, she moved into a straddle, feeling his erection nuzzle against the damp furrow of her sex.

Max kept himself in good shape at 36, although gray had started to creep into his dark, curly hair. He had an easy smile, one that charmed her in the first place, but was almost infuriating to look at now.

"What am I going to do with you?" she asked.

"Love me?"

"Always, Max. Forever." She touched his face. "I will never gamble this away. I will not put our marriage at risk again. I'm not going to lose you. Lose our family. Our life together. Hong Kong was a total manipulation, yet it could have worked."

"I'm not asking you to gamble. There's no risk. I'm just saying that you should have a good time."

"And I have the *best* times with you, love." She slid backwards, reaching to guide his cock into her.

Max groaned, eyes fluttering shut as she began to roll her hips against his. Was he thinking about her with other men? Or just enjoying the sensation of husband and wife?

He was through sharing thoughts, Katie realized. He knew when to push, and when to hold his tongue. He also knew how dangerous things could get. He'd shared some of the despair that he'd felt when he thought that she was lost—that she was going to leave him for another man. She never wanted to hurt him like that again, intentionally or not.

She leaned over him, her breasts brushing along the soft down of his chest hair. She kissed the edge of his mouth—along his jawline—into the nook of his neck. She continued to make love to him, her hips rising and falling along his length. He felt so good. So *right*.

Katie squeezed her pussy muscles around his cock, drawing a moan. "Feel this, baby," she whispered. "This is for you. This will always be for you..."

"Katie..." He was close again. She could feel it in the way his heart raced against her breast. Could hear it in his voice.

A wicked thought came over her. A tease. A torment. "No matter how bad I am when I'm in New York, I'll always come back to you."

"Oh, Katie!" Max's body jerked, his hips rising off the bed as he flooded her.

Her orgasm took her by surprise, and not because it had been triggered by Max's. In the breathless instant just before orgasm, she was back in the alley, pinned against the wall, being ravaged by a man whose name she didn't know.

CHAPTER 2

Over the next month, the conversation passed into memory. Her new job didn't involve nearly as much travel as her old one had, so she had no trips to New York to tease Max with—and he didn't bring it up.

Despite the fact that they'd had sex with two other couples, Katie didn't consider them *swingers*. She'd never think of herself as being in *the lifestyle*. They didn't visit clubs, or search for other couples online. If they spent the rest of their lives exclusively with one another, Katie would have been totally fine with that.

Not that she didn't think about it from time to time. Hanging out with Nadia—a thing that she did on occasion these days—and listening to the other woman recount her salacious nights with other men had a way of getting Katie's imagination going.

"Hey, remember that guy you hooked up with in New York?" Nadia asked.

Katie had met the attractive Indian American to discuss what they'd wear to the upcoming Halloween party. Nadia had quickly decided that they'd dress up as harem girls, then launched into the latest tale of torrid, illicit sex. Situations like this no longer seemed strange to either of them, although six months ago, Max's coworker had felt like Katie's archrival.

"The guy in New York? It wasn't really a hook-up. Just a kiss."

Nadia smiled knowingly. "Riiight. Well, I think I hooked up with him last week. And it *wasn't* just a kiss."

Despite herself, Katie felt jealousy tighten in her gut. She suppressed the irrational emotion. "Yeah? How do you know it's him?"

"You seem awfully calm."

Katie forced a laugh. "How should I react? It was so long ago. I didn't even get his name."

"AJ," Nadia said, her smile almost infuriating.

"What?"

"That's his name. And I know it was him because Tatyana introduced us."

"As in owner of The James?"

"Yeah. John was up in New York on business. I tagged along. Ended up hitting up The James, then...AJ."

"You little slut."

"You're just jealous."

Katie laughed. "Maybe."

"Well, you should be," Nadia said. "The man could fuck. At one point, he had me begging for him. Me. Begging!"

"You really are a slut," Katie said, shaking her head.

"I am, and I'm not ashamed to admit it. You should try that sometime."

"What?" Katie asked.

"Letting go. Just giving in to the urge. You've heard me say it before, but the beauty of a fuck buddy is that you can be anyone you want to be. He's not going to judge."

Katie felt heat well up inside her before she could help herself. Dark thoughts of fucking other men invaded. As always, the memory of her time with Greg—the only time she'd been with a man without Max there—assaulted her. She'd been such a slut then. Such a whore. He'd called her as much. Had used her. He'd forced her to her knees, ordered her to blow him, then came all over her face. She'd never told Max that detail because she hated what he'd think of her.

Yet shamefully, the act still turned her on.

"You're thinking about it now. Aren't you? I can see your nipples through your blouse."

Katie ignored her and buried her thoughts. "Was John there? That night with...AJ?"

"Actually, the husband wasn't. Would you believe that he turned in early? Something about having to get up the next morning."

"Some of us work normal hours, Nadia dear. Not all of us are bartenders."

"Bar *managers*," Nadia corrected, swatting Katie's arm.

"Forgive me. Bar managers who go into work at...what time again? Noon?"

Nadia ignored her. "Anyway, John encouraged me to head out to The James."

"I'm sure he did," Katie said, thinking of how Max would have done the same.

"When I got there, your boy, AJ, was there as well—"

"He's not *my boy*," Katie interrupted.

"Well, he should be. He's got an amazing body. Really, really fit—definitely your type."

Katie blushed. She never should have admitted that to Nadia. The woman seemed to tease her every opportunity she got.

"Seriously, Katie, he may be one of the best I've ever been with."

"Wow, that's saying quite a lot," Katie teased.

"I know, right? His muscles aren't the only thing big and hard."

Katie blushed.

"Like I said, he actually had me begging. Not even John has been able to do that."

Katie had quashed most of the jealousy, but now envy took its place. She rubbed her thighs together, putting herself in Nadia's place. "Sounds...fun."

Nadia pulled out her phone. "Want to see some pics? We took some for John that night…"

Katie wanted to say no. She really did, despite the pique of curiosity she felt. But before she could find her voice, Nadia was already thumbing through the photo gallery on her cellphone. Katie caught glimpses of blurred flesh and dark hair. She averted her eyes, color springing to her cheeks.

"You really let him take photos?" Katie asked. "What if they got out on the internet or something?"

"Only way that would happen is if John stuck them up there, and he's not going to do that. I only let guys take photos with this," she said, turning the phone around and sliding it in front of Katie. "He has such a good body..."

Katie wasn't a fan of the upward trend in mobile phone screen sizes until she saw AJ's torso displayed on the 5-inch screen. The photo was of a man's tanned and toned upper body, from his neck to just above his pubic bone. He had zero body fat on him, seemingly constructed of muscle and sinew. Just as she'd imagined, he was built more like a swimmer or soccer player than a body-builder.

"Sorry about the headless nature of it," Nadia said. "It was part of the deal."

She flicked over to the next photo and Katie gasped. The first had been hot in a GQ way. The second was just plain pornographic. It was taken from the man's downward looking perspective—Nadia on her knees, naked, her hand wrapped around a large, erect cock. The raw sexuality of the image took Katie's breath away. She studied it as she would a painting in a gallery. The thick cock had an upward curve like a scimitar, capped by a fat head that Katie could practically feel rubbing across her g-spot. He had no hair at the base, only smooth, dusky skin that made the whole thing even more obscene. In the photo, Nadia was studying it with an unadulterated excitement that bordered on worship—a feeling that Katie could almost relate to.

Nadia flicked the photo to the next frame, this one showing her lips stretched around the huge cock. Her cheeks were hollowed out, her almond-shaped eyes staring up at the camera through thick lashes.

Katie's heart raced like she'd been sprinting. She could practically feel that thing in her mouth. She tongued the top of her mouth like it was AJ's girth. Her pussy tingled, wet. Her body burned.

"Pretty hot, huh? God, he was big," Nadia said. She flipped to the next photo. Katie's jaw dropped a little. Again, the POV was the man's. This time he was laying back, the angle capturing the muscular sweep of his abs, right on up to Nadia's naked body. She was straddling him, her body arching up and away, her flawless skin glistening with perspiration.

Katie was drawn to their union, where his cock was buried to the hilt inside her friend's neatly groomed pussy. Somehow, that made it look even bigger.

"Okay, I get it. Thanks for the anatomy lesson," Katie said, pushing the phone away. She wondered if Nadia noticed how her fingers shook.

Nadia picked the phone up, flipping through some more photos with a smile. "I've got more if you want to see. There's a pretty good one of him fucking me from behind that makes my ass look fantastic."

"I bet." Katie laughed. "No thanks."

"So now look me in the eyes and tell me you don't want some of that?"

Katie looked at Nadia, fully intending to tell her just that. But she just couldn't. Instead, she dodged the question. "Fine, he's hot."

"And he's here in DC."

"Wait, what?"

"Yeah, he's *here*. He's a personal trainer over at City Fitness. Last week, he was just visiting New York. He actually moved down here shortly after you two hooked up—"

"Kissed—"

"Denied your impulses," Nadia finished. "So he's been here all along."

"Wait 'til Max learns that juicy little detail." Katie laughed again. "It'll drive him crazy."

Nadia raised an eyebrow. "Just him?"

Katie's heart pulsed. She thought about the kiss—how he'd manhandled her, holding her against the alley wall. She thought about those photos, then shook her head before a blush overwhelmed her. "Yeah, just him." Katie barely believed it herself.

"Uh huh," Nadia said. She leaned back in the booth, brushing her fingers through her loose, dark hair.

"What?" Katie said, feeling defensive. "Don't do that."

Nadia shook her head. "Do what? You're the one living in a state of denial."

"I'm not. Don't get me wrong, I still think about the bartender... AJ, was it? What it would be like to be with a guy like that. Like I said, he's hot. But I also think about Max and how he'd react."

"Katie, I'm not here to pressure you into anything," Nadia said. "I'm not Chloe..."

Katie snapped out of her defensiveness. The woman sitting across from her *wasn't* Chloe. She may have been just as beautiful, and certainly just as sexual, but she wasn't a schemer. She was her friend, and she would always put Katie's best interests first. Any ulterior motives of Nadia's were entirely about bringing more "fun" into her friend's life. They just happened to disagree on how to define "fun."

"I'm sorry, you're right," Katie said at last. "But I made a promise to myself never to do anything to risk what I have with Max."

Nadia nodded, clearly biting her tongue.

Katie followed her logic—mostly because she'd also been down this road. All she needed to do was recall her conversation with Max from a couple weeks ago. He'd told her she could have slept with AJ back then, without his permission. He'd told her that would have been sexy. She ignored the memory, forging ahead.

"Look, I'm just not ready to go there," Katie said. "Maybe one day we'll be as comfortable with that as you and John, but I don't know..."

"Fair enough," Nadia said. "More for me if I don't have to share him with you."

Katie laughed, although she still felt the twinge of irrational jealousy. "Pretty sure you'll still be sharing him with others."

"You've got a point there..." Nadia fingered her phone, then said, "So you really don't mind?"

"If you saw him again? God, no. I mean, I didn't even know his name until now." Katie said it almost as much for herself as for Nadia. Then, she joked: "Why? You have a date lined up with him tonight?"

Nadia bit her lip, looking down, then back at Katie.

"You do!" Katie said, more surprised than anything. "With him? With AJ?"

She still didn't associate the name with the man, and it was easier to think about Nadia fooling around with AJ than the guy she'd encountered in the alley.

"Well, I was out already. You usually turn in early. So I figured, why not grab a drink with him?" At least Nadia had the grace to look sheepish.

"When?" Katie asked.

Nadia checked her phone, then flashed Katie a wincing smile. "In about five?"

"Calling things close." Katie chuckled wryly.

"You're welcome to join us," Nadia offered, more as a consolation than a genuine offer of a threesome.

"I'm going to pass. But thanks." She reached for her wallet, pulling out a credit card. "Split the tab?"

"Hey, Kates, you're not upset, are you? Because seriously, I'll tell him to fuck off if you'd like. He's not worth our friendship."

Katie softened, once again reminding herself that this woman was a friend, not a rival. This was why she always got along with guys over girls.

"No, have fun. I'm sorry I'm being...weird." She tapped Nadia's phone. "Don't let a cock like that go to waste because I kissed the guy once upon a time, and have no intention of doing more."

"You're sure you're sure?" Nadia asked.

She wasn't. "I'm sure."

But she *wasn't*.

"Then let me pick up the tab. The rest of my drinks will be on

AJ, anyway."

"Have fun tonight, whore," Katie said with a laugh.

"Have fun wishing you were me. Night, Kates."

That statement was packed with so much truth that Nadia had no idea. Or maybe she did.

On her way out, Katie passed AJ. Or a guy who approximated the memory she had of him. He'd grown his dark hair out and buzzed away the sides, but the rest was how she'd remembered—same broad shoulders, same broad and broken nose, same self-assured smile.

As they passed, their eyes met. He regarded her with confused recognition, unable to place her but sure that they'd met. She nodded and smiled back, then slipped out into the night, pleased with herself. If he'd not recognized her at all, she would have been hurt. If he'd placed her immediately, she would have been mortified.

She pulled out her phone and started a text to Max.

–you'll never believe who I just ran into...

CHAPTER 3

"So his name is AJ?" Max asked with a smirk.

They were sitting at the kitchen table, drinking coffee the morning after she'd been out with Nadia. Light poured in through the large bay windows, filling their recently remodeled kitchen with light.

Max had come home after she'd gone to bed. So the conversation had to wait until the next day, which was unfortunate for Max since Katie was so horny that she was ready to explode.

"Yeah. He's apparently an AJ," Katie said.

She'd filled him in on most of the details. He'd listened quietly, asking only a few clarifying questions. Katie got the distinct impression that she was proving to a disillusioned kid that Santa Claus was indeed real.

"And you just ran into him?" He scratched the side of his face. "Huh..."

"What?"

Max shook his head, reaching for his coffee. "Nothing. Just seems so...convenient is all." He sipped, but the smirk remained.

"You don't believe me!" Katie said, putting it together.

"No, no, it's not that." He laughed. "Well, I kind of don't."

Katie laughed with him. "Whatever. It doesn't really matter what you believe."

She stood and went to the counter to refill her coffee—feeling his eyes follow her as she did. She'd worn her black satin nightgown with the white lace fringe.

"So are you going to see him?" Max asked, although she wasn't sure whether he was humoring her or not.

She poured her coffee and added cream, thinking about how to answer that. The truth was a resounding *no*, of course, but she was pretty sure Max didn't want to hear that. Holding her coffee to her lips, she blew across the steamy surface. "Maybe I have already..."

It was a lure for her husband, but he didn't bite immediately. She could see the giddiness he was trying to hide behind his ever-calm demeanor. "Go on," he said.

She watched him watch her. He observed her as a stranger would—as AJ would. She could practically picture herself the way a new lover would: tall, willowy curves, creamy skin dappled with freckles, sheathed in a satin slip negligee that did fantastic things to her breasts. The short hem just barely covered the tops of her thighs, and even her husband seemed to be willing it shorter.

Katie shivered with excitement. She set her mug behind her, leaning back on the counter, her hands clutching the edge.

"Maybe when he saw me, he recognized me... Stopped to say hello. Invited me to stay with him for a drink."

"Maybe he did," Max said. "But what about Nadia?"

"Oh, you know Nadia. She's a good friend. Made some excuse to leave us alone." Katie wasn't sure that's how it would go down, but when she saw the cloud of doubt fall across Max's face, she wondered if he actually believed her. "And when we were alone… Well, things picked up just where we left them."

"You found an alley to make out in?" Max's jovial nature had begun to falter.

"We didn't need to. The booth was private enough."

Max rose, pushing his shoulders back and puffing out his chest. He worked out when he had time and had a nice body—not as nice as AJ's, she couldn't help thinking, but comparing him to a personal trainer's physique wasn't fair. He wore a t-shirt and a loose pair of pajama pants, which were tented with his excitement.

"I can imagine it was," he said. "Did he kiss you?"

"Mmm hmm."

He stepped close, wrapping his arms around her tenderly. It was comforting, having him so close. She could smell the coffee on his breath. She could see the flecks of gray in his day-old beard.

"And you let him?" he asked.

"Want me to show you how?"

She leaned in and pulled his mouth down to hers. Their lips crashed, opening to one another, tongues ready to unfurl. She balled her fists in his shirt, feeling his body heat beneath her knuckles.

He kissed her back, just as hungrily. Was he thinking about her with another man? Yes, of course he was.

Something about that inflamed her. She hated it. Hated that he had that kink, and yet she couldn't stop help teasing him about it.

Max broke the kiss. He grabbed her by the hips and turned her to face the counter. A window looked out on their quiet street. The gauzy white curtains gave them enough privacy, but this close to them, she could see the world beyond them. A couple walked their dog down the other side of the street. Mrs. Thompkins was working the flowerbeds in her front yard as usual, despite it being October.

Behind her, Max lifted her negligee to her hips. He touched the smooth petals of her pussy. She was soaking. What did he think about that?

She moaned as he sank two fingers inside her. She bent forward, bracing herself on her elbows. She felt his free hand on her tailbone, holding her steady as he started fingering her. He knew exactly how to touch her, how much pressure she liked, and how to twist his fingers to get her off. Her body rippled with pleasure. She loved how well Max knew her body.

"What are you thinking about?"

You, she didn't answer. He didn't want the truth right now, although she almost gave it anyway. Instead, she pushed his buttons as surely as he was pressing hers.

"Comparing your technique with AJ's—" A moan cut her off. He curled his fingers across her g-spot, his thumb rotating around to play with her clit.

"And?"

"He's good. Different. Harder."

Max fingered her harder. She bit her lip, feeling an orgasm build. She imagined AJ's powerful body behind her, finger-banging her, calling her a slut for wanting it.

"Yes..." She moaned, turning the word into a multi-syllabic warble.

Yes, but no. She didn't want that. She wasn't a slut. She was a woman who'd one day be like Mrs. Thompkins out there, sturdy in her old age, with a rich and full life behind her.

AJ's fingers left her for a moment—no, Max's fingers. Her husband's. She protested, reaching behind her to bring them back. She was so close. Her fingers found his cock instead, erect and ready.

"Let's compare something else," he said.

She helped him guide his cock against her pussy. He entered her with ease, filling her like no other man could.

"You feel so good, baby," Katie sighed. "So big!"

She wasn't lying. He felt fuller than usual, turned on by the fantasy.

"As big as your lover?" he said. He let her get used to his cock with slow, languid strokes, when all she wanted was for him to take her.

"No," she said. She thought of the photos on Nadia's phone. "No, he's bigger."

The truth just came out, and only when it did, did she hear how bad it sounded. She braced herself for the hurt to follow, or the anger. Instead, Max clamped down on her hips and drove himself deep, hitting spots that he normally couldn't reach.

"You like bigger, don't you?" Max's voice felt like it was hundreds of miles away. The man entering her, fucking her, pummeling her g-spot with each thrust, was not him. Was someone else. Greg, for a moment, then AJ with all the muscles she'd seen on Nadia's phone, with that glorious cock shaved bare like some porn star.

Katie hung her head between her shoulders in those last moments before her climax. Her hair shimmered around her, the auburn catching in the morning sun. Mr. Thompkins had joined his wife, knotted hands clutching a rake as he set about dealing with the leaves. Traffic began to pick up as families started their Saturday morning rituals.

Katie saw none of it. Behind her tightly shut eyes, she was consumed with the stretch of AJ's glorious girth, and the way he rammed it deep, again and again.

She took one last breath before her orgasm crashed through her, turning her world on its head. She felt his come flood her, hot and so naughty. So profoundly wrong.

Her moan seethed through her clenched teeth. Her face scrunched up, a grimace that embodied everything that she felt about this fantasy—pain, disgust, and lust despite it all.

The orgasm subsided at last. Max withdrew with a groan from them both, and he was Max once again. She clutched the kitchen counter, uncertain that her legs would support her. Max was there, wrapping her up in his arms, holding her close.

"I love you so much, babe," he said.

Even through the haze of her orgasm, she felt her anger flare up. Anger that this fantasy made him love her more. Anger that he had the fantasy at all. Wasn't she enough? Why did he want more?

She kept those thoughts to herself.

"We should probably go pick up Mya from your parents' house," she said instead.

"Right. I'll go. You take a shower."

Further conversation on this subject could wait for another day.

CHAPTER 4

But that day wasn't the next day. Or even the next week. Life returned to normal. Or normal-ish, anyway.

Max managed his bars, which were doing very well. He was considering opening another Callahan's, possibly in another city, but hadn't given it much thought beyond a what-if.

Mya had started kindergarten, which seemed crazy to them. Katie joined the PTA at her school, and wondered every time she attended a meeting what dirty little secrets the other moms had—some of whom were attractive in that affluent suburban way.

At work, she began an audit with a new client—a nonprofit without a big staff but with a surprisingly complex ledger. She typically worked from her office, but a few clients like this preferred that she work on premise. She didn't mind it as long as it didn't require her to travel—a deal-breaker for her. It let her get out of the office and change things up.

Change things up. Was that really what she was looking for? The past year had already been a whirlwind. She didn't think that she could take any more change, and yet she couldn't look at a good-looking guy without wondering what he was like in bed. It didn't help that most of those guys looked at her the same way.

"We've put you up in one of our smaller conference rooms," said Bradley Spencer, the CFO for IMBARK. "It's not big, but you have a window."

"Don't worry about me," Katie said. She glanced at Bradley as he led her through the office—a surprisingly well furnished space for a nonprofit. Bradley had nice shoulders and a nice head of hair. She put him around her husband's age—late thirties, maybe forty. She wondered if he worked out, then forced herself to think of anything *but* that. "I was once given a closet as a work space. As long as I have access to coffee, I'm good."

"Oh, we've got you covered there." He waved at a break room along the back. "We've got a Keurig machine in there, piped into a water supply. And of course there's the Starbucks downstairs."

He led her down a hallway lined with offices. "Here we are," he said, opening one of the last before the hall turned the corner. "Your home away from home."

Bradley wasn't kidding about the size. It wasn't a closet, but it couldn't have been large enough for more than three people to squeeze into. That said, the window was nice.

"Nice view," she said, setting her satchel on the small table and going to the floor-to-ceiling window.

Bradley stepped up beside her. She wore heels, but the CFO still towered above her, his shoulders even with her eyes. She liked that.

"I like it, too," he said, confusing her for a moment. Had she spoken aloud? Her face went red before she realized that he'd been talking about the view. "It's a nice reminder of why we work in the city."

IMBARK was on the corner of the block, occupying the third floor of the new, all-glass office building. The conference room looked out over the perpendicular street from the one she'd entered. Shops and restaurants lined the broad avenue, and just across the street was the downtown location of City Fitness.

Katie's heartbeat jumped. Wasn't that where Nadia said AJ worked? She scanned the second floor, where tall windows allowed her to look right into the row of treadmills that looked out on the same street.

"City Fitness. That must be convenient," she said when she didn't see Nadia's lover.

"It's a nice facility. They've recently renovated it, too. I could probably get you a company discount if you're interested in joining."

That was an intriguing but dangerous thought. "Thanks, but I actually prefer yoga studios to the gym."

She felt Bradley's eyes sweep over her, managing to keep her smile to herself as she pretended not to notice. "So let me go get my computer and I'll show you where we keep all of our files," he said.

"Sounds good," Katie said. He started to leave when she stopped him. "Bradley? Could you also bring some coffee?"

"Of course. Anything else?" He smiled at her. She wondered what he'd think about her if he knew the dirty things she'd done— and then wondered if he had any secrets.

"No, I'm good for now." God, she really needed to get her thoughts under control.

****

Her job at IMBARK was pretty standard. Most of the grunt work had already been done by a team of junior accountants. As a senior manager, she was responsible for reviewing the work papers.

Nonprofits could be tricky in the way they reported things, and she'd run into more than a few situations where contribution accounting got dicey. Some nonprofits also played fast and loose with the reporting of their investment portfolio, particularly in a down market at audit time.

So she'd look over the work papers, ask Bradley, or one of his assistants, to bring her the paper trail detail if the notes were less than clear, and she'd make sure everything was kosher. It wasn't the most stimulating job—especially when doing it alone—but Katie didn't mind it. There was something comforting about looking over numbers and making sure everything added up.

And the window into the world outside helped pass the time.

That first day, as she got acclimated, she watched people come and go, up and down the street, working through their own problems, their own dramas. She watched a man argue into a phone as he stomped down the sidewalk—was it a business deal gone wrong? A cheating spouse? Maybe he was just trying to get out of his cable contract? She watched a young couple eat their lunch outside, despite the crisp chill in the October air, only with eyes for each other. Later, she watched the wait staff take in all the chairs so that they wouldn't have to serve outdoors.

She found that most people were on their phones, their world reduced to a tiny piece of glass held two feet from their faces. They weren't talking—not in the traditional way—and if they were being social, it was of the Facebook or Twitter variety. Call her traditional, but she never got into social media. She had a Facebook account, of course, but rarely checked it and never updated it. Max did, both for his businesses and for personal updates, and she depended on him for news on friends she'd long forgotten.

She wondered if AJ was on Facebook. She even went as far as

browsing the City Fitness website, in search of his full name, when Bradley walked in.

"Decided to check out the gym after all?"

"Um, yeah. Just looking to see if they have day passes." Katie felt like she'd been caught looking at porn.

"I think they do."

"Thanks." She minimized the browser window, hoping that he hadn't noticed that she was on the staff page.

"Everything's in order?" he asked. He had this reassuring attitude that made her wonder if he had something to hide.

"So far, so good." She gave him a list of things she needed.

Once he was gone, though, her attention drifted back out those windows and across the street. City Fitness was right there, a stone's throw away. AJ could be working his shift right now.

Again, she scanned the second floor with all those cardio machines—the ellipticals, stationary bikes, and treadmills. Mostly women rode them—women in tight workout clothes and with even tighter bodies. Of course a guy like AJ would work at a place like that.

She pulled up the City Fitness browser window and closed it without looking. Back to work. She was done thinking about AJ.

****

But of course, that was a lie. On Tuesday, she took the long way around the block so she could pass by the front of City Fitness on the off-chance that AJ was also just arriving.

On Wednesday, she even packed her gym clothes, telling herself that she was just "keeping her options open."

Max saw the black duffle on her way out. "You find a gym close by the client?" It was a totally innocuous question, asked with half of a piece of toast in his mouth.

It left Katie bright and mortified. "Um, yeah, I might give the place across the street a try."

"Have fun. Love you."

On the way in to work, she puzzled out why she hadn't told Max that AJ worked there. Max would have been all for it. That was inherently the problem. He'd be too into it. It would have been like throwing a raw steak in front of a starving dog. She had no intention of doing anything, so it wouldn't have been fair to get her husband all excited.

So she told herself.

She ended up not going to the gym after all. A complication arose instead, a problem with contribution accounting that started small and ended big.

Bradley wasn't happy, but not for the reasons she'd expected.

"Damn it, I told them that we couldn't classify all those contributions as non-restricted." He looked visibly upset.

"Who is *they*?"

"Our board of trustees. They all think they're business geniuses. Some are. Most are just lucky."

"This happens more than you think with nonprofits," Katie said. "But you need to go back to your board and get them to approve some reallocations. I'll get you a report by close of business."

"Thanks, Katie. You're a life saver."

Turned out, "close of business" was just before nine that night. Bradley stayed with her, keeping a steady stream of coffee and paperwork coming.

"Done," she said, pressing Send on her Outlook and leaning back into her chair. Even when not looking at her computer, she saw numbers and calculations flitter across her vision.

"Great. Reviewing now." Bradley sat with her in the little office, working on the PowerPoint that would have to go before the board. He'd arranged an emergency Webex the next morning, and she hoped he'd be rested enough to persuade them. It would be bad for all parties if he couldn't, but she knew how stubborn some boards could be, particularly if the treasurer and president weren't used to being questioned.

Katie swiveled in her chair, casting her attention back across the street. Back to City Fitness. It closed late—eleven or so—and was all lit up at night. The cardio machines were mostly empty. A few women were on the ellipticals. A guy was running. And pacing just behind the row of machines was the man she'd been searching for all along.

AJ.

He looked good, even in the electric blue polo that the staff wore. Despite the distance, she could appreciate how it clung to his powerful physique. His dark hair was as it had been when she passed him at the bar—longer, molded back, buzzed on the sides. He had no visible tattoos, which both appealed to her and surprised her.

He could see the women watching him in the reflection of the windows, which must have looked like mirrors from inside the gym. He watched them right back, pausing to say something to each. Katie rolled her eyes at their reaction. *Giggle, giggle, no I'm not doing anything tonight... Giggle.*

"Sluts," Katie muttered under her breath.

"Excuse me?" Bradley asked. She was suddenly back in the conference room—back in *Katie the accountant* mode.

"Sorry, nothing."

Bradley craned his neck to look outside anyway. Katie's face burned, although there was no way he'd know what she was looking at.

"This place turns into a shit show at night. Even on a Wednesday," he said, looking at the street.

Katie noticed the clusters of people drifting down the street, heading from the Metro to the bars. The women wore tiny skirts and tall heels, while the guys got away with jeans and untucked shirts—Katie could never figure out how that was fair.

"Lots of douchie bars and clubs around here."

Katie laughed. Starlight Lounge, one of her husband's, was just a few blocks away. She wondered if Bradley considered that a *douchie bar*, but didn't ask.

"Kids these days," she said instead.

Bradley laughed and went back to the report. Katie went back to AJ watching, although the trainer was no longer in sight.

"This is perfect," Bradley said, closing his laptop. "You're good at your job."

"Thanks," Katie said. "I like to think so."

He checked his watch. "Wow, it got late. Can I get you dinner at least? I know a great restaurant around the corner that's still serving."

She knew that she probably shouldn't accept—Bradley was a client and going out for dinner this late had the appearances of being bad—but her stomach was grumbling and she figured it was harmless. She'd already called home to wish Mya goodnight, and she had to eat, so she accepted.

"Non-douchie restaurant?" she asked, grabbing her things.

"There are a few," he said, cracking a smile.

"Lead on."

****

On the way, she sent a quick text to Max, telling him she was grabbing dinner with the client.

–have fun!

It was hard not to read the implication in that reply. She started to text something defensive back, but decided to put it away instead. Let him stew.

The restaurant Bradley brought them to, Brasserie 99, was a Belgian restaurant that was on the upscale side.

"Sit at the bar or in the restaurant?" Bradley asked.

Katie looked at the bar, which was loud and packed. "Let's sit in the restaurant. Kind of noisy over there."

As soon as they were seated in the quieter restaurant side, she wished she'd chosen the bar. She'd had meals with clients many times—some even as good-looking as Bradley Spencer—but never over candlelight. This felt like a date.

Bradley picked up on her discomfort immediately. He laughed as the waiter handed him the wine menu and ran through the specials. "Want to move?" he asked, looking at the bar.

"No, this is totally fine." She was being silly. It was. And the food looked great.

The meal was delicious. They shared drinks and conversation. Bradley was as charming as she'd suspected he would be. She learned that he was divorced, although he didn't offer details and she didn't ask. He had no kids, lived in Maryland, owned a dog. He was a genuinely nice guy, and Katie didn't bother lying to herself—she could easily picture herself sleeping with him.

The really crazy thing was that she probably could have if she wanted to. Max would support her—would even nudge her along that path—and she wouldn't be a homewrecker or anything. The possibility of an indiscretion was exhilarating.

Not that she would. Part of her resistance had to do with him being a client, of course. She didn't like crossing that professional line. More so, Bradley was the kind of guy she could settle down with if she was single. He was handsome, successful, intelligent. But she already had one of those guys, and Max was irreplaceable.

Now AJ...he was a different story.

"So tell me about him," Bradley said.

"Him?" She colored, thinking of AJ.

"Your husband? Or is there someone else?" The question was lighthearted and mostly a joke...mostly. He was fishing.

"My husband's a great guy. Next year, we'll celebrate our ten-year anniversary, if you can believe that."

"Congratulations. You must have gotten married at fifteen."

Katie tucked a strand of hair behind her ear. "Thanks. Twenty-one, actually, but I might as well have been fifteen. No one gets married that young anymore."

"That's very true, but hey, you're still married. I got married when I was thirty and it only lasted a couple years. What's your secret?"

She thought about the crazy things she'd done the last year, laughing nervously. "Communication, right? Isn't that what they all say?"

"Something tells me there's more to that story than you're telling me."

Katie shook her head. "There is, but that's all you're getting."

"Woman of mystery. Intriguing."

"Aren't all of us accountants?"

She was rewarded with a laugh.

"Hey, I better get some sleep tonight," he said. "I've got an important presentation to the board tomorrow."

"Yes, you do."

Katie picked up the tab, despite Bradley's protests. "Don't worry, you'll be paying us a lot more than the price of a meal and a few glasses of wine."

Bradley laughed. "Yeah, you'll add twenty percent and include it in your billing."

****

Katie got home just before midnight. She was pleasantly surprised to see the bedroom light still on. Spending the day with her fantasy man across the street, coupled with the nice dinner with Bradley, had her worked up enough that she was going to have to deal with it, Max or no Max.

She stepped into the room to find Max propped up in bed, playing on his phone.

He put his phone down and looked at her, practically brimming with excitement. "How was…dinner?"

Dinner. She heard the suggestion. The innuendo. It transformed the sweet night into something sordid; it turned her mild flirtation with Bradley into something to be ashamed of.

"Dinner was good. Brasserie 99. We should check it out sometime." She went to her dresser and began to remove her earrings.

Aware of him watching her as she undressed, Katie took her time unfastening the buttons that ran the length of her black dress. She glanced back in time to catch his hungry expression as she shucked it off, leaving her in her black bra and thong.

She heard it—the quick intake of breath.

"You're wearing stockings?" he asked.

She bent over to touch the lacy tops of her nude, silk stockings. "All my pantyhose had runs in them."

It was the honest truth, although she saw how he read into the lingerie choice—she was out unexpectedly late with a strange man, and her lingerie suggested certain things.

"Were those in your gym bag? Or did you put them on for your date?" he asked.

Of course, the gym bag. He'd read the wrong thing into that, too—that it carried things for some illicit affair—although the truth of that bag wasn't much better.

"No, I wore these all day."

She released her hair from the clip that had been holding it up all day, shaking it out in loose, auburn waves.

When she turned back to him, his phone was on the bedside, forgotten, and his arms were folded behind his head. He looked good like that—the well-formed peaks of his chest stretching out the tight, v-neck undershirt. She remembered how horny she was.

But it was the way he looked at her that really got her going—like he wanted to possess her, to ravage her.

"Does that turn you on?" Katie asked, crawling onto the bed, still in her lingerie. "That I wore my thigh-highs all day long and no one ever suspected?"

Max's voice came tight. "No one?"

"Maybe Bradley suspected something. We spent almost all day together..."

She crawled over him, dragged the soft lace of her bra along his chest. She could feel his heart racing, even through the undershirt.

"He the guy you had dinner with?"

"The CFO. Yeah. You'd like him. About your age. Successful. Smart." She grabbed the bottom of his shirt and pulled it over his head. Tracing the sparse crop of curls between his pecs, she said, "He's fit, too."

Max reached behind her, twisting open the clasp of her bra. "I bet he was looking at these all day," he said, tracing his fingers gently over her full breasts before teasing his her nipples, drawing a sigh. "I bet you teased him."

She hadn't, but Bradley had looked anyway. Her nipples hardened even more at the memory.

Katie kissed her husband, pushing thoughts of Bradley away. She didn't need him to want *this*. She stripped out of her thong as Max pulled down his boxers. He was hard. Ready. She wrapped her hand around his girth and placed it against her pussy. She sank onto it, wet and welcoming.

Biting her lip, she stifled the moan, but it came anyway. Max felt right. Perfect. Familiar. Those weren't bad things. She wasn't restless for more. She didn't dream of gigantic cocks plundering her depths.

Katie grabbed the headboard, bracing herself over Max. His mouth found her tits, sucking on her nipples as she undulated on his cock.

"Katie... Katie... You feel so good. You're so...hot..." The word got swallowed in a groan. He grabbed her ass, squeezing it, urging her to ride him faster.

It easily could have been Bradley beneath her—Bradley's strange cock buried inside her. Bradley wanted her. She could have him. And even though she knew she'd never do it, she had permission to play.

"Who are you thinking about?" Max pulled her down to him, nipping at her neck.

"You," she lied.

"You're not. I can tell, baby. You always fuck me like this when you have someone else in mind."

Like this? She had a tell? She tightened her fingers in his hair, burying her head in the pillow behind him. She concentrated on Max, on his smell, on the heat of his body, on the way he grunted with each thrust. She knew this feeling. These sensations. He felt like home to her, her base, her sanctuary. All it took her was the memory of Hong Kong and how close she'd been to losing this and she'd always find strength to resist guys like Bradley.

"I'm thinking of *you*, Max. You're all. I. Need."

She ground her hips harder into his in response to her inner demons, taking him as deep as he'd go as her orgasm rushed up around them. Together, they sank into those dark waters, lips finding one another, his balls tightening, his heat filling her world. She wanted to stay here forever, lost in the tangle of his arms, his legs, his familiar embrace.

But she couldn't. The world moved on, and so must they.

Rolling onto her back, she stared up at the ceiling as Max sidled up beside her. He fingered the lacy top of her thigh-high. "I like that you sometimes wear these," he said.

"I bet you do."

"Goodnight, Katie." He was already half asleep.

"Night, dear."

Katie didn't follow. Not immediately. She laid awake, wondering why she hadn't told Max that she'd been thinking about Bradley. Was it shame? Embarrassment? It troubled her, but not enough to hold sleep at bay forever.

She needed to watch that. She told herself to remember that when she woke. But of course, like always happens, the thought was gone by morning.

CHAPTER 5

"We're all going to happy hour after work," Bradley said the Friday following the big accounting debacle. "And I definitely owe you a drink. Join us?"

The presentation to the board had gone well. Bradley's best weapon had been the report prepared by Katie, which the board members took more seriously than the advice of their own CFO. It would mean extending the contract with Katie's firm a little to sort it out, but Katie was kind of looking forward to the grunt work. It had been a while since she'd had to prepare work papers.

Plus, she liked this company.

"Sure, happy hour sounds great."

"Great. It just got a hell of a lot better for me," Bradley said.

"And don't think you're going to get away with a cheap domestic lager with me."

"Of course not. I don't think there's anything cheap about you."

That had been how it had been between them these last couple days. She could feel the growing sexual tension between them, and even knowing that nothing could happen, it was still exciting. She got up Friday morning looking forward to it, choosing her outfit specifically with Bradley in mind.

IMBARK had a casual Friday policy but Katie made it a habit to maintain her professional image, so while everyone dressed down in jeans and sweaters, she still tied her hair up, wore a suit, and pretended like it was any other day.

Today's suit was tight and black. She didn't wear it often because of how tight the pants clung to her, but the thought of Bradley's eyes on her ass every time she walked away was too tempting. The top was cinched high on her waist with a white belt, emphasizing the hourglass lines of her otherwise lean body.

She'd made sure that Max saw what she wore beneath, walking out of the bathroom in the black padded bra and g-string. He hadn't said a word, but he didn't need to. He approved.

Friday proceeded like the other days she'd spent in that little room. She reviewed documents and papers. She drank coffee. She gazed across the street at City Fitness.

She still had her gym bag with her, sitting in the corner of the conference room, unused but not forgotten.

Katie hadn't talked to Nadia since the evening they'd gone out for drinks and Nadia had eventually met up with AJ. Had that turned into more? Most likely it had, knowing Nadia. Katie wondered if he was as good the second time as the first. She found herself staring into the cardio room again, and had to shake her head to clear it.

IMBARK knocked off an hour early for their happy hour. Katie told them that she'd meet them there because her hours were billable, but Bradley waved it off. "I'm the money guy. Don't worry, you're covered."

They went to Lucy's, a tiny basement bar that Katie only knew about because her husband was in the bar industry. As flashier bars came and went, Lucy's existed under the radar, small, slightly divey, but always charming.

"So what'll it be?" Bradley asked. Ten of them from IMBARK came out, mostly from Bradley's team, but there were a few others mixed in. "Bud Light?"

Katie cracked a smile. "If that's what *you'd* like. For me, I'll take a vodka martini."

"With a twist, or dirty?"

Which would you prefer? Katie almost asked before she remembered herself. "Today feels like a twist of lemon kind of day."

"Twist it is."

Being married to a bar owner, Katie was no stranger to the bar scene—the noise, the tight confines, the conversation over drinks. But most of those times, Max was nearby, or she was in the company of his colleagues. This was different. It felt like her own thing.

They mostly stuck to IMBARK-related topics and gossip, but it was still fun to listen to. They asked her about her opinion on things as an outsider. She gave it when she could while remaining neutral. Apparently their CEO was an asshole who wanted to run the place like a for-profit corporation—which incidentally led to the misallocation of revenue that Katie had to untangle.

Occasionally the conversation would shift to Katie and her life. "You have a five-year-old? I can't believe that!" one of the guys said, slapping his hand on the bar top.

"Why not?" Katie said with a smile. She was fishing for the compliment, but it still warmed her to hear it.

"Well, first of all, you don't look like a mom at all—" he began to say when Bradley cut him off.

"What Steve here's trying to say is that you're so professional and pulled together that it's hard to believe that on the weekends, you're driving a minivan around."

"That's not what I'm saying!" Steve interrupted. "I'm saying most moms I know are frumpy and stopped giving a shit about their appearance. Let's be honest, here. Katie, you're a babe."

Katie covered her mouth and laughed.

Bradley put his arm around the junior accountant. "And you're drunk."

"Pretty sure that goes for all of us, boss," another guy said.

Bradley ignored the comment, although judging from the blush in his cheeks, Bradley was feeling the drinks, too. He turned to Katie. "He has a point, you know. You don't look like you should have a kindergartener at home."

"And how should I look? Sweats and a ponytail?"

"I believe the MILFs wear yoga pants now," Steve blurted.

"I think that may be the first time I've been called a MILF," Katie said. "To my face, anyway."

Even Bradley laughed.

"We didn't plan on having Mya. I was just 25 and in career mode, but life doesn't like following plans."

Bradley nodded thoughtfully. Thinking about his own divorce, maybe?

"And I bet your husband couldn't keep his hands off you," Steve said, going for a high five that no one reciprocated.

"But you know what? I don't regret any of it. Mya is awesome. Life is different, but I can't imagine it without her anymore."

The conversation settled down after that. The IMBARK crowd thinned and Lucy's filled up. Time flowed with the drinks, and before Katie knew it, it was pushing eight and she was firmly buzzing.

"How did it get so late?" Katie laughed, checking her phone.

"Something about having fun while flying?" Bradley said.

"Oh, shit, look at that," said Steve, the only other guy from the office left. "I promised to meet my girlfriend a half hour ago. She's gonna be pissed." He threw some cash down and was out the door with a nod.

Bradley chuckled. "She'd probably be more pissed if she knew how much he kept checking you out."

Katie was too buzzed to be embarrassed. She'd noticed Steve's eyes dipping to her cleavage every opportunity that he thought he had. She'd noticed Bradley doing the same.

"You don't have a leg to stand on there," she said.

At least he had the grace to look chagrined. He looked down at her tits, which peeked out over the top of her black jacket thanks to her padded bra.

"You can't honestly blame me." He stepped back, holding his hands out. "But to be fair, go ahead and return the favor."

Katie laughed, but took up his offer. Bradley's version of Casual Friday was exactly how she'd expect a finance executive's to be: a golf shirt tucked into a pair of khakis. He did fill the golf shirt out well, though, and once again her imagination went to hot and sweaty places.

"Very nice, Mr. Spencer. I'm sure you do alright."

That's when she noticed him. Like fate. The crowd parted. There was a momentary break in the din of the bar—enough for her to hear a familiar laugh. She looked, and there he was, dressed in a t-shirt and a pair of worn jeans.

AJ.

Her body trembled like this was some kind of celebrity sighting. Her heart rate spiked. She hated that he made her feel like a fifteen-year-old girl. The crowd shifted again and she saw the woman that he was chatting up—petite, pretty, and blonde. That helped suppress the giddy palpitations she was having. Did she really want to be like that blonde?

She didn't dare answer that.

"Hey, you there?" Bradley asked. He glanced over his shoulder to try and identify whatever she was looking at.

Heat burst across Katie's face. "Yeah, sorry. Thought I recognized a girlfriend over there."

Bradley turned back to her, oblivious to AJ. "So, Katie, I've really enjoyed working with you. You're sharp. You're capable. And you're not so hard on the eyes."

He delivered the last statement with a light-hearted laugh, but Katie wasn't drunk enough to miss the nervous look beneath. He was working up to something. She cut him off before he said something they'd regret in the morning.

"Thanks, Bradley. You're one of my easier clients." It was a subtle reminder of their relationship, but it was enough.

He nodded, understanding the rebuff. "Let's see what next week uncovers." He pulled out his wallet. "Time for me to close the tab and head home...unless you want another?"

Katie waved her hand. "I've had enough. For sure. Thanks for the drinks, Bradley."

She suddenly had the urge to kiss him on the cheek, but resisted. Instead, she looked around as he waved down the bartender.

Katie looked back at the spot that she'd seen AJ. He was still there, although the blonde was gone. *Looks like you struck out tonight,* she thought with a smirk.

"Okay, the bill's paid," Bradley said.

"Oh, I was going to offer to pick it up." Katie refocused on Bradley.

"You were going to pay for the drink I owed you? Doesn't seem right."

"Well, I think I had a few more than just the one." She picked her purse up, fishing out her phone again. Max had sent her a text.

–hope you're having fun

Katie smiled, knowing exactly where her husband's mind was. She couldn't wait to get home to him. He wouldn't know what hit him.

"*It's about to get a whole lot better,*" she texted back with a giggle.

"Cabbing it?" Bradley said as they moved out into the night air. They pulled on their long coats, their breath clouding in the chill.

"Yeah."

For a moment, she wondered if he was going to offer to split a taxi—and where that taxi would actually take them. She looked up at him through her lashes as he slipped on a pair of wrap-around earmuffs.

He hailed a taxi, and when it pulled up, he opened the door like a gentleman. She imagined him sliding in after her. Imagined him wrapping his arm around hers and pulling her in for a kiss. She shivered—and it had nothing to do with the cold.

He didn't follow her in. Instead, he held the door and smiled. "It's been a real pleasure working with you, Katie."

"You too. Have a good one, Bradley."

****

Katie and the taxi nearly made it out of the city when she realized that she didn't have her gym bag. She considered leaving it there—she could pick it up in the morning, or worst case, buy a new set of workout clothes.

But the in the end, the prudent side of her won out. "Sir, could you turn back? I forgot something at the bar."

The taxi driver shrugged. He didn't care. The meter would run up no matter where they went.

Traffic was thicker heading into the city than out. It was funny. The bar scene was just beginning to heat up, and she was well beyond ready to be home. Her wild days of bar-hopping felt like another lifetime.

And yet parts of her life were wilder than ever.

Even alone in the back of a cab with the night flashing by, she blushed. Not exactly the white picket fence lifestyle she thought she'd have in her thirties. It made her wonder what things were going on behind everyone else's fences.

She arrived back at Lucy's just as a line had begun to form. The bouncer recognized her and let her through.

As she stepped back into the bar in her dark suit and the coiled hair, she felt heads swivel in her direction. She saw herself through their eyes—a happy hour straggler on a Friday night. Someone who didn't quite belong.

She hurried to the bar where she'd been standing all night, but her bag wasn't there. Disheartened, she waved the bartender down.

"Excuse me. I think I left my gym bag here. Did someone turn it in?"

He looked at her like she was speaking another language. She began to repeat the request when someone tapped her on the shoulder. "This what you're looking for?"

She knew that voice without needing to look, even though she'd only heard it once. She recognized the gruffness, the New York accent, the confidence. It was AJ.

She turned to look, her heart skipping ahead of her.

"Yes. That's it." *Did he recognize her?*

He grinned. "You seem to make a habit of leaving things in bars."

She didn't know whether she should feign ignorance. Would admitting that she remembered him make her appear weak?

"Do I know you?"

AJ saw right through the deception. He reached out, and for a second, Katie thought he was about to draw her in for a kiss and flinched. Instead he leaned against the bar beside her, their bodies only inches apart now.

"You do."

Katie squeezed her thighs together, holding her breath as she half turned to face AJ pressed next to her.

"How did your presentation go? Back in New York?"

"It went…it went well."

"Did you have one here, in DC? Or is this home?"

Katie considered lying, but realized that wasn't going to work. "This is home."

"Well, that's convenient. Same here."

This close, he looked even better than she remembered. His tight black t-shirt clung to his upper body in a way that made Katie want to tear it off. He still had the nose that looked broken, yet somehow perfect on him. And she still really, really wanted to climb into bed with him.

He held up the gym bag. "Working out around here?"

Katie blushed. "I was thinking about it. I've…I've been working for a client around the block, and noticed the City Fitness." Her confidence grew as she spoke. Her heart rate started to calm. "I just never had the time to get away, you know?"

"I know that story. People never make their bodies a priority."

He traced her own body, first with his eyes, then with his hand, resting it on her hip.

She should have pushed him away. Instead, she looked around to make sure no one recognized her.

"You look like you make time for your body, though." He said drew her attention back to him. "You should have come over. I would have loved to help motivate you."

Katie would have liked to think that in any other circumstance, she would have laughed at his forwardness—that it was the drinks that had dropped her guard.

"Come over where?" she asked. She wasn't supposed to know that he worked at City Fitness—that she looked for him every day from her perch in that little conference room.

AJ laughed to himself. "You realize that I can see as easily through your windows as you can see through mine, right? And I'm a sucker for the sexy corporate look."

Katie's face went bright red. She wanted to curl up under the bar.

"Were you looking for anyone in particular? Or just letting your…mind wander?"

"Can I have my bag please?"

"Want me to give you a tour of the facility? I have a key. It can be very private."

The suggestion registered like fire between her legs, and she hated herself for it. "My bag?"

"Don't I get a reward?"

Katie grabbed for her gym bag, but he pulled it behind him. Suddenly they were face to face, her body pressed to his. Worse, the crowd shifted, pushing them even closer.

He smelled clean. He must have showered at the gym before

heading out, and that thought naturally brought the image of him in the shower, suds racing down the muscled contours of his naked body. The fire between her legs grew hotter.

He was tall and sturdy. She had to lift her eyes to meet his. She didn't realize that she'd grabbed his shirt to steady herself, and let go as soon as she did.

"You know, you're kind of a bully," Katie said.

"It was just a question," he said. "How about your number?"

"I don't think so. I'm married, remember?"

"Then you buy me a drink?"

Katie sighed. She knew he wasn't going to back down from this one. "Fine. What do you want?"

"I'm easy. Bud's fine."

Thinking back to her conversation with Bradley, Katie almost laughed. Of course he'd drink Budweiser.

"Weren't you working in an upscale cocktail bar the last time we met?" She flagged the bartender down and ordered the cheap beer for AJ and a glass of water for herself.

"Worked there. I didn't drink there."

Katie suddenly got the distinct impression of what AJ must have thought about that clientele. It made her self-conscious. "You think you're better than us yuppies?"

AJ grinned. "You said it, not me. But no, it's not that." He laughed. "Well, not really. Has more to do with where I choose to spend my money. A $15 cocktail isn't it."

His drink arrived. She handed his to him and left some cash on the bar, intending to get out of there as soon as she could. "So where *do* you choose to spend your money?"

"Thanks for this," he said, downing a third of it. True to his word, he handed her the bag. "Rent, mostly. This city's expensive."

"And the rest? Dates?"

"I don't date much." He seemed to get a kick out of messing with her.

"Seducing married women?"

AJ's laugh felt genuine. It even brought a smile to Katie. "That's not as expensive as you think."

"You're unbelievable." Yet she couldn't stop smiling.

"Most women tell me that I'm *amazing*, but I've heard unbeliev-able, too. You sure you don't want that private tour of the gym?"

Katie set her glass of water on the bar and shouldered her gym bag. "Enjoy the beer. AJ."

"Don't I at least get to know your name?"

Katie smirked. "No, I don't think so."

She couldn't stop smiling all the way out of the bar.

****

Katie buried her face in the pillow, her moans more growls than cries. She raised her ass higher, changing the angle of the cock pounding her from behind. So good. So full...

She turned her head enough to breathe, her red hair spilling across her face, sticky with sweat.

She imagined AJ on his knees, taking her doggy style. AJ's hands on her hips. AJ's cock driving deep, stretching her out.

"Harder." Her voice cracked. "Harder!"

"You're so sexy, babe," Max groaned, his voice faltering under the strain.

The illusion cracked. Her husband was back, giving her what she needed. Doing everything right.

"Come, Max. I want to feel your come."

"I'm close. I'm so close..."

Reaching between her legs, she danced her fingers across her clit, pushing herself over the edge. She clenched her teeth and crashed through her orgasm. A moment later, Max was there with her, flooding her, filling her, overflowing and dripping down her thigh.

She collapsed into a puddle of mush in the mattress, ass still up, hair a tussled halo around her.

Max stayed semi-erect, despite the orgasm, rubbing his hand across her ass cheeks. He always liked her butt, and it was nice to think she still had it, even after all these years.

He withdrew with a shared groan. "So who were you just with?" he asked.

Katie's face went bright. Her throat constricted. She sank into the mattress, but didn't turn around. Didn't even open her eyes.

Max helped her out. "Bradley, was his name? Bradley Spencer from IMBARK?"

At last, she turned on her side and looked up at him. Max lay down beside her, brushing a damp strand of hair from her face.

"Doing some research?" she asked.

Max looked sheepish. "I couldn't help it. I wanted to see who it was making a play for my wife tonight."

Katie's body warmed, even through the glow of her climax. "And?"

"So you're not denying that he was?"

Katie bit her lip coyly. "I'm not."

"I can definitely see your type. A little older. Successful. Well-dressed. I bet he was respectful, even as he was trying to get with you."

"He was..." Max had Bradley pegged. He was all of those things. It made sense. Bradley was a lot like Max, and she *was* attracted to that type.

But then she thought of AJ. AJ was nothing like that. He was exactly the kind of guy she should hate—a cliché for a rich girl to crush on. Was that what was happening? Was she living out this cliché at thirty years of age?

"Go ahead and keep thinking of him," Max said, rolling her onto her back. He was hard again—not fully, but enough to sink into her damp sex.

Katie tried to bring Bradley's image to mind—tried to indulge her husband's fantasy—but AJ kept imposing himself. She could almost smell his musk. She spread her legs, willing Max to dominate her the way she imagined AJ would.

"At least part of you wishes this is where your night ended," Max said as he began to fuck her. "I can feel your excitement. Your nipples...they're so hard."

He rolled the hard points with his free hand. She arched her chest, pushing her full swells into his palm. Behind her eyelids, she imagined AJ squeezing them, roughly pawing at them.

Max was gentler than that, but he knew her body well enough that it didn't matter. He could play her like a virtuoso, teasing out a moan even as she wanted something harder—rougher, more aggressive.

She grabbed his hand and guided it into the balmy space between them. He took the hint, although she sensed his surprise. He found her clit at the base of her landing strip, flicking it as he slid in and agonizingly slowly out of her.

"This what you wished he'd done to you?" He fingered her button, sending wave after wave of pleasure through her body. "Or maybe this is what he did?"

Max picked up speed as his own fantasy formed. His hips thrust harder. His fingers circled her clit with purpose.

She encouraged it, even as their fantasies diverged. "Yes," she whispered. "Yes, just like that..."

"He got you somewhere dark. A corner booth, maybe," Max said, the narration broken by his heavy breathing. "He kissed you. His hands wandered."

She imagined AJ's lips on hers again, aggressive, demanding. She laced her fingers through his thick hair, pulling him closer. They were back in the alley in New York, making out against the brick wall. This time, his hands wandered and she didn't stop him. They slid across her ass. They slid inside her pants—inside her thong.

"Did he like what he discovered?" Max asked. He pulled at the closely cropped hairs of her strip. "Was he surprised that such a proper woman kept herself like this?"

Is that what Max really thought? Was that why he got so excited about how she groomed herself?

"Yes," she hissed. "He...he loved it. Called me...called me a dirty girl..."

She liked that. Liked the ring of it. Max did, too, taking her harder.

"Oh, yes, Katie. You're such a dirty girl. So..." He moaned. "So..." Louder. Closer. Harder. "So fucking bad. So...so..." The rest was lost as he came, ramming himself to the hilt as he went off inside her.

Katie clutched at his head, drawing him against her shoulder as she folded her legs around him and pulled him close. She sank her teeth into her lower lip, stifling her own moans. She didn't come, but it felt good enough that she was fine with that. She held her husband as he sighed and finished inside her. Visions of AJ were gone. They were back in their bedroom, and the fantasy was just that again.

Max rolled off of her and went into the bathroom to grab some tissues. He brought a wad back to her, and she smirked at how practical this part of their sex was.

"That fantasy really gets you, doesn't it?" Katie said once they were settled in. She still felt the buzz of her martinis—enough that she had the courage to be truthful. "I like it, too."

Max was quiet for a long time—long enough that she wondering if he'd fallen asleep on her. When he spoke, though, his voice was clear. "Doesn't need to be a fantasy..."

She almost gave the standard response: *Yes, it does.* But they'd had such a good night—good enough that she could entertain that possibility again.

"It doesn't always need to be like Chloe and Greg. Not all guys are that sinister. We mostly just want to get laid."

"I know." She did. Max and John were good guys. Trustworthy guys. They were safe.

Safe. That was kind of the problem. Bradley was safe. AJ was not. And who couldn't she get out of her head? Who was the one she really wanted to fuck?

And what did that say about her?

"Look, I love you so much," said Max. "And the way you tease me—like tonight, or Wednesday with that late night dinner date—or any of it...that's all enough for me. It's more than enough. That you're willing to tease me like that at all is just awesome." He ran swirls across her thigh. "But you should know that if you ever wanted to do more than just tease me, I'm open to that, too."

"But Hong Kong—"

"Was Hong Kong. I thought you were going behind my back. Now I know that you'd never do that."

"I wouldn't."

He snuggled close, kissing her on the top of her head. "Honestly, it's just sexy knowing that you're out there, up to no good."

"So what are you saying?"

"I know that you didn't do anything with Bradley tonight. I know that you were just teasing me. But..." He hesitated. She finished the sentence for him.

"But I could have if I'd wanted to." She looked at him. "Wouldn't you want to watch?"

"I would, but...but I don't have to. The idea of you out there—"

"Being naughty."

"Being naughty," he agreed, "is so hot. That's enough."

This whole conversation felt familiar. They'd been down this road before, and it hadn't ended well. Before she could help herself, she called it how she saw it. "Bullshit."

Max stiffened. "What?"

"Bullshit, Max." Katie's body shook with the adrenaline of the upcoming confrontation, but she needed to call a spade a spade. She rose up. "I know what you're doing and you need to stop it."

"Stop what? I don't know what you're talking about."

Katie ran the conversation through her mind before stepping into it. How do you tell a confident man that he was overcompensating due to a lack of confidence? Truth was, the last time they'd tried this open lifestyle, it had nearly destroyed them. It had certainly destroyed his confidence in her. For one fleeting moment, Max had believed—truly believed—that she'd cheated. That was hard to come back from.

"I think that your excitement is clouding some deeper...emotions." She almost said insecurities. It was the correct word, just not the appropriate one to say aloud. "Hong Kong happened. I hate that it did, but we can't ignore how that *changed* things."

Max was stony faced. He was processing it all. She went on.

"It turns you on thinking about me fooling around and being

naughty, but at the same time, deep down, I *know* that it scares the shit out of you. I've seen it. We've been there, Max. Not to rehash the same conversations again and again, but I think we need to move past this point."

Max didn't say a word for the longest time. He just lay there, looking at her but lost in thought. Katie knew him well enough to let him think it through.

"You're right," he said at last. "So what do we do about it? Do you want to call it quits?"

That would have been the easiest solution, but it was also the laziest. "I don't."

She felt Max's cock stir. He was so predictable.

"But we should establish some ground rules," she said.

Max groaned. "You know, you don't have to wear the accountant hat all the time."

"This one's more my Type A personality one." She laughed. "And yes, I do."

"So ground rules," he said. "How about we keep it simple. Nothing is planned, but everything is shared afterwards."

"Sounds perfect." Katie straddled him, kissing him softly. He was being so good, he deserved a little tease. "And who knows, maybe I'll be too busy being naughty to tell you right away."

She thought about AJ then, and he could easily make her feel naughty enough.

As if on cue Max said the words that would haunt her in the weeks and months to come.

"No barriers, Katie. Nothing's forbidden."

"That's a bold statement," she said.

"I'm a bold man." She hugged her close. "A bold man who trusts his wife."

They made love for a third time that night, but the fantasy talk was over. As their bodies undulated in the dark, their minds were on the unknown ahead.

CHAPTER 6

"I feel naked," Katie whispered to Max. She tugged at the veil across her nose and mouth. It didn't conceal anything, but she could pretend it did. Not so much for the rest of her harem girl costume.

Max looked her up and down, lingering on her overflowing cleavage. "You look amazing."

She dug her elbow into his side. "It's not fair that you get to wear all those robes and I'm basically wearing a bikini."

"Hey, you and Nadia were the ones who decided I should be the sultan." Max was dressed in the black and gold robes of an Arabian Prince, complete with a brocade fabric headpiece featuring a plume and a jeweled diadem.

"I'm now convinced that Halloween was invented by a man," she said.

"A genius," Max agreed with an infuriating nod. "And don't tell me that you didn't have fun last year."

Katie grew hot at the thought. Last year, Max had arrived late to the bar, leaving her at the mercy of costumed, horny men. When he finally did arrive, *he'd* pretended to be one of those costumed, horny men, and they'd ended the night fucking in the parking lot.

In the back of both of their minds, they were probably thinking of how this year could top that. It was probably why Katie had agreed to wear this ridiculous costume. The turquoise spangled top was no bigger than a bra, hung with golden chains; the baggy genie pants were as transparent as her veil and featured open slits up either side; the tall, golden sandals with their spindly, golden heels highlighted her perfect feet and red painted toenails. She tugged again on the veil, feeling the eyes on her.

"Look, there's John and Nadia," Max said.

Their friends were on the opposite end of the room, laughing with one another as they sipped drinks from Jack-O-Lantern Solo cups. It was nice to see them happy together. It was even nicer to see familiar faces. This was a house party thrown by friends of Nadia's; Max and Katie knew no one.

As they approached, Katie studied her old colleague, John Mitchell. To complete the theme, he was the sultan's guard. He wore a brocaded vest that left his arms bare, along with a crimson fez on his head and Roman legionnaire style sandals. He looked sexy—and so very different than in the business suits that she was used to seeing him in. Her mind jumped right to sex and the one evening they'd shared after The Katherine had opened.

It happened every time she'd seen him—not that she'd seen him much. Since they no longer worked for the same accounting firm, and he was still in New York, they'd only gotten together once or twice socially since that fateful night.

"You made it!" Nadia said, spotting them approaching. She appeared buzzed already. "And damn, girl, you look hot."

"I can't believe you talked me into wearing this," Katie said. "I can't pull it off like you can."

Nadia's costume was a black and gold version of Katie's, only where Katie in a harem girl outfit was definitely a costume, Nadia actually pulled the look off with her deep golden skin and shimmering black hair. She'd added a jeweled belly piercing that dangled in the center of her flat stomach and matched her earrings. A golden bangle wrapped around her left bicep.

"Please, no one's looking for authenticity," Nadia said. "They just want to see skin. Right, John?"

Katie looked at John just in time to see him pull his eyes off her chest. That sent a flash of heat through her.

John's smile was almost shy. He shrugged, and said, "It's Halloween, after all. And she's right, you look great."

Katie's mind flashed with an image of John stripped naked except for the fez as she bobbed her lips along his length. Her pussy quivered.

"Thanks. You don't look so bad yourself," she said. "How are things, by the way?"

"Good. Still stuck in New York, but I've got a lead on something."

"Oh?"

He'd been talking about getting out. He and Nadia had been splitting time between New York and DC, and while the two cities were four hours apart and the couple had an open relationship, Katie knew her friend well enough to see how hard it was on him.

"Yeah. Too early to even talk about, though," he said.

"Well, if there's anything you need from me, let me know."

Nadia snickered at that. She'd sidled up to Max, a hand on his arm. She whispered something into Max's ear, which caused him to smile and nod his head. They looked so chummy. Katie felt jealousy spike through her—a reminder that no matter how secure she was with her marriage, she'd never be as comfortable as Nadia and John were with an open relationship.

Not that she couldn't trust Max. Nadia had worked for Max for over five years and they'd always been close and flirty. It used to make Katie nervous. Now, Katie had no reason to be; Nadia loved John too much, and Katie knew Max loved her.

"Max and I will get drinks," Nadia said. "You two get caught up."

Katie started to object when John said, "Come on, I'm going to grab a smoke. Keep me company."

Katie glanced back at her husband, who gave her a subtle nod. *Go, have fun,* he seemed to say. She knew him well enough now to know that he was getting turned on by the possibility of a repeat of their foursome.

Katie linked her arm into John's. "Lead on."

They went out onto the balcony, which was empty. It was warm for late October, but she was still wearing next to nothing. She half considered going back in to get a drink to warm her.

"Smoke?" John asked.

That would do. "Please."

She only ever smoked when she drank, and only then very rarely, but the idea of hot smoke in her lungs, along with the buzz that accompanied it, sounded tempting. She was too sober to be with this man alone.

John took out a cigarette, lighting and handing it to her. Sharing a cigarette felt bizarrely intimate, even though the last time they'd been alone was when they'd cabbed back to her house after the opening of The Katherine, torn each other's clothes off, and fucked each other silly.

She was still amazed that she'd done that. She sucked down the smoke to calm her nerves.

"So how're you doing, Katie?" John asked. Katie looked up at him, not seeing her longtime friend and former coworker, but instead seeing him as the last man to fuck her besides Max. He added, "Things better with the new firm?"

Katie blinked, reminding herself who he was. A friend. Just a friend. She handed him the cigarette.

"Yeah, much. It's a smaller accounting group, so we all wear more hats, but I don't mind the grunt work from time to time. Reminds me why I became an accountant."

John nodded, smoking the cigarette as he watched her thoughtfully. Their eyes met. "You're basically good at anything you put your mind to."

"Same with you." Her heart skipped in the pregnant moment.

He handed the smoke back to her.

They stared at one another, smiling and comfortable.

Katie had always liked John. He was the opposite of an alpha male—the kind of guys who she found herself drawn to lately. He was on the other end of the spectrum, the consummate good guy. The kind her parents would have been happy for her to marry. She'd always liked him for that, but the more she got to know him, the deeper that appreciation became. He was strong when he needed to be, stubborn about things that he was passionate about, and more ambitious than his introverted personality suggested.

He was also fantastic in bed, she thought, her stomach once again doing flips.

She held the cigarette to him. His fingers lingered against hers before he took it. She remembered the way he'd kissed her so many months ago. The way he'd held her hips as he made her scream. That didn't help with her nerves.

She forced the conversation to more appropriate things. "You and Nadia still doing okay? With the whole long distance thing and all?"

"Yeah. Better than most couples in our situation, I bet."

"Well, you've got a pretty unconventional way of dealing." Katie's face went bright red. She was far too sober to have this conversation, yet here she was, spewing freely.

"Everyone's different," John said. "How about you two? How are you guys doing?"

"Great," Katie said, maybe a touch too quickly. "All things considered, I mean."

"You two had a bad experience. That's not easy to get over—especially when it's one of your first."

Katie nodded, filling the silence with a final drag of the cigarette. She dumped the butt into an empty beer bottle. "Life's kinda crazy and unpredictable, isn't it?"

John looked at her, their eyes meeting in the dark. She no longer felt chilly. "Very," he agreed.

The moment was interrupted by the sliding door opening and the ruckus of the party spilling out. "Should we come back?" Nadia said.

Katie stepped away from John—when had she gotten so close? Turning, she saw Nadia in the door and Max just behind her. She saw the conflict in her husband's face—the same conflict that she felt when she noticed that his arm was around Nadia's waist and his hand was on her bare midriff.

"We come with gifts," said Nadia, holding out some drinks. "But if you two are having a moment—"

"No, of course not," Katie said. "Drinks. Yes. Thanks."

John lit up another cigarette. When he offered it to Katie, she shook her head. She was always self-conscious about smoking around Max. Drinking was a better buzz.

"What is this?" she asked, guzzling the punch too quickly.

"What do I look like, someone who works in a bar?" Nadia joked.

Max added, "It'll get you buzzed. Does it matter?"

"You two run an upscale speakeasy that specializes in artisanal cocktails?" Katie said. "Very interesting."

Nadia rolled her eyes. "Just drink, snob! You're way too sober."

Katie laughed and did as she was told

****

The night flowed along with the booze. Katie hadn't been to a party like this in a long time. The apartment was packed to standing room only. People clustered everywhere, dressed in outlandish costumes that made Katie feel better about her own—it was like every male fantasy had come to life. Sexy maids and nurses were represented. A sexy teacher danced with a sexy school girl across the room. Cheerleaders and vampires and slutty versions of Disney princesses all mingled through the tightly packed throng.

Katie and Nadia were in line for more drinks, and had to yell to be heard. "So have you seen that guy again?"

"AJ?" Nadia asked. Katie nodded, as if she didn't know exactly who AJ was. "Yeah. Couple times. I invited him to this, but he had other plans."

Katie's heart lurched at the bullet she hadn't realized that she'd just dodged. Not that she had anything to hide, but meeting AJ at a party like this could have been awkward.

"How about you?" Nadia said. "You got any guys in your bullpen?"

Katie laughed at the analogy. "No one warming up, if that's what you mean. But there's a guy."

It was a testament to how strong the drinks were that Katie said anything at all. Nadia's interest was piqued.

"Oh? Anyone I know?"

"No. Just a guy I'm working with."

"Client?"

"Yeah," Katie said.

"Katherine Callahan is mixing business with pleasure?" Nadia faked a scandalous tone. "I'm shocked."

"I know. And it's nothing, just some fun."

Nadia pinched Katie's arm. "I'm just teasing. I think it's great. And shows how much you've changed over the last year."

"Well, a lot's happened."

Nadia pressed herself close to Katie, her fingers curling around the redhead's waist. "A lot, yes."

Katie inhaled Nadia's perfume, distinct, spicy, and undeniably feminine. She suddenly became hyper-aware of the other woman's warm hands on her bare skin.

Nadia leaned in, her voice gentle, barely audible above the ruckus of the party. "It still makes you nervous, doesn't it?" Nadia tilted her head, as though preparing for a kiss. Instead, she smiled and added, "But I know you like it."

Katie's chest felt tight. The two times she'd been with another woman had been in the context of group sex—in the heat of an already intense sex scene. This felt different. There was no way to deny her attraction.

Katie started to protest—more out of good girl instinct than genuine concern—when Nadia completed the action she'd started moments before. She dipped in and kissed Katie on the mouth.

Katie's body stiffened. Nadia's nose brushed along her own, her lips and mouth so unbelievably soft. Panic yielded to excitement—the same thrill of being a bad girl, of being unexpected.

The women melted into one another. The party around them faded away. Even the feminine body pressed against her lost definition to the sensual play of tongue against tongue.

Nadia broke the kiss. The world around them came crashing back. The guy behind them dressed as a Jedi cheered a big, "Don't stop now, honeys!"

Katie's face burned.

Nadia said to Katie, "Want to get out of here? I bet John and Max are ready to leave, too."

Katie did, but it scared her. She hadn't realized how much baggage she'd been carrying around since the Chloe thing—since Hong Kong. She'd nearly lost her husband and her marriage because of that mess, and right or wrong, she tied Nadia and John to it.

"Come on, ladies, don't tease a guy like that," the Jedi said.

Nadia turned to him. "Would you shut the fuck up? Go beat off somewhere else."

"Whoa. Princess Jasmine's got a temper on her," he said, hands up.

Katie couldn't help but laugh. Nadia grabbed her hand and pulled her out of line. Katie just looked back at him and shrugged.

Nadia drew Katie into the bathroom, which surprisingly had no line. As she locked the door behind her, a thrill passed through Katie.

"For privacy," Nadia explained.

Instead of going right in for another kiss, as Katie expected, Nadia leaned against the sink and looked Katie in the eyes. "I know you're still marked by what happened. I respect that, and if you want to go back out there, find Max, and go back home with him alone, I'll totally respect that, too."

Katie felt sincerity in Nadia's words. She wasn't Chloe—she wasn't trying to seduce Katie into doing something she didn't want to do.

"But?" Katie asked, finally relaxing.

"But I want to fuck you so badly," Nadia said, letting it all out in a breathy rush. "And so does John."

Katie laughed. Giggled even. What else could she do? She wanted all of it. No sense in denying it anymore.

"Okay," Katie said.

"Okay?"

"Yes. Okay, let's go find the guys."

****

They all piled into a cab, heading to Nadia and John's place. Max sat up front, John, Nadia, and Katie crammed into the back with John in between the girls. Everyone was buzzing, and it was from more than booze and nicotine.

Katie turned to John, her earlier shyness snuffed out by the electricity of the night. "Hi," she said.

"Hey, yourself," was all he could manage. Katie kissed him hard, cupping his smooth cheeks as she cradled his head. It felt good to kiss a man—reassuring to her sense of heteronormativity.

Not to mention Max, there in the front seat, watching her do it. That lit a fire inside her.

Breaking the kiss, she glanced at Nadia, waiting eagerly opposite her. "Your turn," she said, directing John's head around to his wife's. The two kissed deeply, tongues meeting in a wet duel.

Katie looked over at Max, who was twisted around in his seat, mesmerized. The cab driver was, too, although he only risked furtive glimpses in the rearview mirror as he drove them through the night.

An audience. She had an audience. Her breathing sped up. Her body hummed.

John pulled out of his kiss with Nadia. "Your turn?" he said. At first, Katie thought he was going to kiss her again, but he sat back in the seat, put his hands on the back of the back of Nadia and Katie's heads, and nudged them together.

Neither needed much prompting, although again Katie had to fight back her reflex to pull away at the last second. As Nadia's lips found hers, and Nadia's tongue sliced into Katie's mouth, the instinct to flee dissipated. She welcomed the kiss, reveling in it.

Still, subconsciously maybe, her free hand sought out John's cock, finding him erect and ready through his loose pants.

Katie squeezed it, felt it throb. She couldn't wait to feel that inside her again, she thought guiltily.

When Nadia and Katie separated, Katie realized that the cab was stopped. They'd arrived at Nadia's condo complex. Max paid the driver. Said: "Thanks for the ride."

"Buddy," the driver said, "I think your ride's about to start."

"I think you're totally right."

****

Katie bobbed up and down John's length, indulging in the strange cock like an exquisite meal. She loved the way it felt in her mouth, how different the contours were as she traced it with her tongue. Most of all, though, she loved the way he groaned above her as she blew him.

As *they* blew him, she corrected. Nadia was on her knees beside Katie, her mouth focused on John's balls as Katie sucked his shaft.

John groaned. "Oh, fuck yeah, that's good."

Nadia pulled up. "Switch," she said.

They switched, Nadia going to work aggressively sucking John off as Katie dipped low and slathered his shaven balls with saliva. When she wrapped her lips around his scrotum and sucked, he moaned sharply.

Katie's pussy quivered. She'd never done this before—never participated in a double blowjob. It felt so naughty. The fact that she was doing it to John, not Max, made it even spicier, albeit with a tinge of guilt.

Nadia pulled up, her fingers replacing her mouth to pump his cock. "So the sultan's guard likes two girls on his dick?"

Katie sucked one last time on his balls before licked up the side of his shaft. When she got to Nadia's fingers, she licked those, too, kissing her platinum wedding band.

Nadia went back to work, lapping her tongue along the opposite side of his shaft, both of them now focusing on his cock. They fell into a rhythm, their lips meeting around his cock, forming a soft, wet ring as they danced up and down his length, two tongues lashing instead of one.

Katie could tell that he was close. His breathing became sporadic. His abs clenched. He moaned harder, louder, squirming under the onslaught. Nadia swallowed him, only to pull away and let Katie take a bob. Back and forth they passed him, each woman taking a quick turn as they tickled his balls with their fingernails.

"Uh, yes!" John groaned, rocking back in the sofa. "That feels... that feels...sooo good!"

Katie's body was on fire, too. Her nipples screamed against the bra-like top of her costume. Her pussy was drenched.

He came inside Nadia's mouth first, although the women orchestrated a perfectly timed switch between ropey blasts of come. Katie swallowed like the sex slave she was pretending to be, passing his cock back to Nadia only to watch the other woman finish him off. Inches from Nadia, Katie was mesmerized. The woman looked so sexy doing that, her cheeks caved in, her eyes closed, long lashes fanning out like half-moons.

When John was through, Nadia released him, turned to Katie, and pulled the redhead into a sweltering kiss. They swapped come as much as spit as they made out. It felt so surreal to Katie. She wasn't the kind of woman who did this sort of thing. What would her friends think of her now, as she French kissed another woman and shared another man's come? What would the partners at her firm do? She thought about her clients—about Bradley—who could never see this side of her.

At some point, the act became less about putting on a display for John and more about enjoying the Sapphic touch. The kiss slowed, their bodies came together. Katie felt Nadia's hand slide into the front of her panties as her own hands cupped Nadia's ass.

"She's so wet, my prince," Nadia said, breaking free to look at Max, sitting on the couch.

Max grinned. He still wore the sultan's plumed headdress and the golden robe, but was otherwise naked. The robe hung open, his cock clutched in his hand.

"Strip each other," Max ordered.

Nadia stood, offering her hand to Katie. Katie took it, letting herself be pulled up and turned to her husband. It was easier to be passive when it was another woman behind her, touching her, working the clasp of her harem girl halter top.

"Just relax, Katie," Nadia whispered. "Look at your husband. He's loving this."

Max was. He was staring with a hungry expression that made Katie shiver. The top came off and Nadia reached around, cupping Katie's full swells. "Do they please you, master?" Nadia asked.

"They do," he said.

"You did well, choosing this slave, master."

Katie saw Max's domineering facade drop for a second and shared a smile with him. The scenario was fun, but also silly, and they knew each other too well to start calling one another *master* and *slave*.

Nadia pinched Katie's nipples, and the silent exchange between Max and Katie broke. No matter how silly this was, that was another woman behind her, stripping her, kissing her neck. There was no way to pretend otherwise. Yet as her nerves set in, she simply had to look at Max, see the hunger in his stare, and she was able to enjoy it.

Nadia's hands left Katie's tits, traveling down her flat stomach to her waist—to the hem of her gypsy pants. Nadia hooked her thumbs into Katie's pants and panties, pushing them over her hips. Katie felt so exposed, even in front of her husband of nearly ten years.

"Keep the heels on," Max said as Katie stepped out of her clothing.

She nodded, then turned to Nadia to return the favor. Nadia didn't turn for her, however, forcing Katie to strip her face-to-face. Katie rolled her eyes at Nadia's insufferable smile, then reached around her and worked open the other woman's top.

Nadia had gorgeous breasts. At just twenty-seven and without going through motherhood and breastfeeding, her olive-hued tits still rested high and plump, capped with dusky nipples that screamed to be sucked on. Katie couldn't resist, dipping in to take one between her lips.

Nadia clutched at Katie's hair, moaning at the touch. "Oh, baby, that's good," she said.

Katie worked her hands down Nadia's lean back, found the waistband of her pants and pushed them downward. Releasing her lip-lock on Nadia's tits, she lowered herself into a crouch to peel down Nadia's flowing pants, putting her right next to the other woman's bare shaven pussy.

Suddenly, everything about this night snapped into vivid, raunchy reality.

Max's voice cut through the roar of blood in her ears. "I want you to eat her."

Katie's stomach tightened, even as her pussy swelled. This felt so wrong, yet so exciting. For the quickest of moments, she remembered the suit-wearing accountant she was by day. Then, she took a deep, fortifying breath, wrapped her hands around Nadia's ass, and ran her tongue across her moist sex.

Nadia moaned, threading her fingers into Katie's hair. Encouraged, Katie did it again, dragging the flat of her tongue across the entire length of Nadia's slit. She was silky smooth. Katie remembered a brush of dark brown hair on her mound, but had to admit the bald look was exciting. Everything that happened was exciting.

Keeping Katie's head against her crotch, Nadia lowered herself onto the sofa, getting more comfortable for both of them. She spread her legs wide, giving Katie complete access.

Katie took it, trying to recall the things that Nadia enjoyed the last time they were together. She pushed two fingers inside the other woman, slowly finger-fucking her as she flicked Nadia's exposed clit. Nadia squirmed, moaning louder, and Katie felt pride warm her insides. She was doing something right.

Katie heard Max speak without fully comprehending the words. "You, there. Guard. I want you to fuck that slave."

Katie continued to eat Nadia's pussy, listening to the other woman's vocal cues as she gauged how close she was to orgasm. Her tongue flashed this way and that across Nadia's clit, a panicked zig-zag that Katie knew felt like magic.

And then she felt something hard and large press against her pussy from behind. She didn't even have time to pull off Nadia's cunt and look back before John entered her.

When he pulled back, the ridge of his cockhead ratcheted up the pleasure a hundred fold. Nadia grabbed Katie's head, shoving it back between her thighs before she could fully wrap her mind around what was happening.

"Don't stop," Nadia moaned. "Keep eating my pussy."

Katie tried, but her attention was divided. She couldn't fully focus on Nadia, not with the feeling of strange cock driving in and out of her. She gave up with her mouth as the waves of pleasure came crashing. She worked Nadia with her hands, finger-banging her with one hand as she worked her clit with the other.

It was enough for Nadia, who finally screamed out an orgasm of her own. She shoved Katie's face back into her pussy, lifting her hips off the sofa, grinding her smooth cunt against Katie's mouth.

And still, John fucked Katie. When Nadia went limp on the sofa, John pulled out long enough to flip Katie over, place her on her back next to Nadia, and enter her once again.

Katie met John's eyes. The link was established. Looking into his deep, brown irises, something dawned on her—something that scared her to death.

She loved this man. The epiphany was as profound as it was obvious.

She placed her hands on his hips. To push him back? To keep him there? He drove into her, filling her, forcing a cry of pleasure from her—and those hands curled around his ass, encouraging him to fuck her deeper.

Vaguely, she was aware of a shift on the couch beside her. Looking to her right, she saw Max there, his robe gone, guiding his cock between Nadia's thighs.

Katie smiled at him, reaching out to hold his hand.

John drove into her again, forcing a moan—forcing her eyes closed and her mind to go haywire.

She loved John, but not in the same way that she loved Max. No one would ever replace him. And she would never, ever let anyone come between them again.

"I'm close," John said.

Katie opened her eyes, looking up at him as he slowed his thrusts.

"Me, too," she said, her voice harsh.

He nodded quickly, picking up speed again, rounding the final bend. He pulled a leg up over his shoulder, opening her wider, driving his large cock deeper than she was used to. He was good. He knew exactly what he was doing. She was so close. Three more strokes and she'd be there. Two more.

"I'm…" The rest was lost in a long moan. She wanted to feel his come, to feel him unleash himself inside her, but instead, he pulled out, ripped his condom off, and exploded across her stomach. The hot splatter of come on her sweaty skin felt almost as naughty.

"That's it, slave girl. See all that come? You're going to clean her up so I can have my turn," Max said.

Max was still in control of the situation, and Katie was grateful for it. She was just a prop in their game, a harem girl who was there only to do as she was told. And she was accepting of that role.

Nadia slid into place between her legs. Max moved in right behind her, a condom rolled over his dick. Katie didn't feel jealousy. Felt no uncertainty. Didn't feel anything but relief and hedonistic pleasure as Nadia went down on her and Max fucked Nadia doggy style.

"I love the taste of come and pussy," Nadia said. She pushed two fingers into Katie, drawing a gasp from the redhead. "And your pussy is so neat and beautiful. I love a tidy cunt."

Nadia went back to work, harmonizing her tongue with her driving fingers. Katie closed her eyes, sparks of pleasure dancing around her in the blackness. Nadia pressed the flat of her tongue against Katie's clit, applying enough soft pressure to keep her sputtering and gasping as her fingers did all the work. Before Katie could fully adjust, Nadia would shift, curling her tongue into a point and working her clit in rapid, flittering strikes.

Katie looked over Nadia's undulating body, at Max taking her like the royal prince he was pretending to be. He still wore that silly hat, although it had been tipped askew.

He mouthed an *I love you*, which she returned with a laugh.

This was the way it was supposed to go down. This was the kind of decadent pleasure the night needed to be, free of heavy emotions. Free of AJs and Bradleys and confusion. Nothing but pleasure in its purest, most unadulterated form.

She looked beside her, where John sat, watching. His cock, she was shocked to discover, had begun to rise again. Viagra had to be at play here. She looked at Max, wondering how much the two men had conspired to get them to this moment. Then decided she really didn't care.

Twisting around, Katie wrapped her hand around his cock and took him into her mouth. She could taste herself on him, along with the residuals of his come. She swirled her tongue, feeling him expand as she sucked. She wanted to feel him inside her again, she realized, complicated emotions or not.

"Oh, Kates, that's so hot," Max said. She glanced at him, catching his riveted expression as she sucked off another man.

Katie slurped away at John, her voice rough from a night of moans and oral sex. "Sorry, babe, I couldn't resist. John's got such a nice, big dick."

Max's face tightened. She knew that expression. It was the anguished look of her husband coming. It felt good that she knew him so well, that she could stroke his emotions like a virtuoso. Nadia gasped between Katie's thighs as she joined Max in his orgasm.

Katie looked up at John, who was staring at Nadia and Max with the same pained lust Max had shown when watching them earlier. She realized she felt the same way. Sliding out from under Nadia, she rolled a condom onto John, turned in his lap, and slotted him into her pussy.

"That's better." She sighed.

John smiled. "Our turn?"

Katie nodded, looking down at Nadia's shaved pussy, red and ready.

"Eat her," Max said. "Make that slave girl come. Your prince demands it."

Katie embraced the harem girl role again. For tonight, on Halloween, she was pleased to serve.

****

Back in their own bed, in their own home, as dawn threatened and sleep loomed, Katie snuggled into Max.

"Did you have fun tonight?" he asked.

Katie laughed breathily. "Do you really have to ask that?"

He chuckled. "I guess not."

"Did you? Did you like watching me with John?"

"Do *you* have to ask that?" Max said back. "Yes, it was intense. You know what my favorite part was? How into it you looked."

Katie felt a pang of guilt at that, especially when he added, "Should I be worried?"

The answer was no, of course. No matter what, no man could ever replace Max. But to blurt that out felt too defensive, which could expose her sense of guilt no matter how unfounded. So she went for the tease.

"I thought you said that nothing was forbidden," she said, tracing circles through his chest hair with her fingers. "Are you now telling me that John is?"

"I said that I trust you. And I always will."

"And you should," Katie said. "I said it before, but I won't risk this." She squeezed him. "I'm not going to risk what we have, right here."

"Good. Neither am I." He kissed her hair as sleep started to take them both. "But I'm sticking by my offer. No boundaries. I trust you."

Katie thought of the possibilities ahead and the freedom he'd granted her. Until that night, she could deny all of it because she didn't think Max could truly handle her having another extramarital fling—sanctioned or not. But he'd seen the way she was with John, the connection they had. If Max was okay with that, then he'd certainly be okay with Bradley.

Or, she thought in the last moments of consciousness, *AJ*...

CHAPTER 7

November rolled in, and with it came snow.

With her newly granted freedom, Katie didn't run out and fuck the first guy who looked at her ass. If anything, she grew even more guarded because of the possibilities. Suddenly flirting wasn't so innocent. It didn't need to stop at a tingling sensation and a laugh—or a phone number that she threw away. She could take any of them home if she wanted.

She'd meet a cute guy in the grocery store who'd sweetly pass her a coupon, and she'd wonder what he'd say if she invited him out to her minivan. Or she'd be sitting across a boardroom table with a client, and couldn't stop thinking about her naked back smeared across the polished wooden surface as he dove between her legs.

She and Max were all over each other, although neither mentioned the new arrangement. Sometimes she'd catch Max looking at her as though wondering if she'd been bad. She'd let him sweat a little before shaking her head with a smile. She didn't miss his quiet disappointment.

Or was she the one disappointed? It was becoming harder and harder to hang this fantasy on Max alone. Not when she'd see a City Fitness ad in the Metro and immediately think about AJ.

Not that he was an option for her. She's already ruled the cocky personal trainer out. Even thinking about crawling back to him—of just happening to show up at City Fitness and asking about him—had her cringing with shame. No, it was best to forget about AJ. Forget about him and every other guy like him. If she was going to do this thing, she was going to maintain her self-respect.

She did think about Bradley Spencer, though, and the chemistry they had. She considered looking him up, although he was technically still a client through the end of the year. She even went so far as to pulling up his number with the intention of asking him to coffee—well, coffee with ulterior motives—but professionalism won out.

Then, at the very end of November, just as the Christmas lights came out and Max and Katie debated the optimal time to buy their tree, she got an early Christmas present.

"So it looks like we need to clarify a few things with the IM-BARK report," one of the partners of her small accounting firm said during the December planning meeting. "Nothing major, but we need someone out there to answer a few questions—"

"I'll go," Katie announced before he even finished.

"That's quite alright, Katie. I don't think you need to go personally. Send one of the juniors."

"I know the file better than anyone." She felt like everyone in the room saw right through her—saw this as the excuse that it was. She soldiered on despite the fear. "Seems best for me to handle it myself."

"Suit yourself. Moving on, we need to discuss end-of-year bonuses..."

****

Katie spent a long time preparing for her return to IMBARK. The day before, she'd scheduled a touch-up waxing with her aesthetician. In the shower that morning, she touched herself, wondering it Max was right—wondering if Bradley would be surprised that a woman like her would groom herself like this.

After washing her hair, shaving her legs, and scrubbing her body clean, she was so primed that she couldn't help herself. Leaning against the tiled wall, long wet hair hanging around her face, she dropped her hands between her legs.

The waxing made her hyper sensitive down there. It was like touching herself for the first time.

Her moans came hushed and fast before she could stop them. "Oh, yes. Uh..."

She focused on her clit, dancing her fingertips on the engorged button. Throwing her head back as she felt a fast orgasm grow, she lifted her left hand to her breast, palming the soft swell. Her nipples screamed, needy and hard, and she tweaked them in time with her clit.

She thought about Bradley doing this to her. Of Bradley standing tall and hard with her in the shower. She squeezed her tit harder, the way a man would. She dipped two fingers inside, simulating his touch. His hand. His cock.

She lifted a foot on the edge of the tub basin, splaying her legs wider. Her fingers dipped and squeezed, and she gave herself entirely to the fantasy. *Fuck me. Fuck me!*

In the flash of her climax, Bradley became AJ. She gasped, but she couldn't stop the flood of her orgasm. It flushed away the forbidden thoughts, but the impression of him lingered.

Breathing heavily, Katie's surroundings slowly returned. The sound of the shower. The pinpricks on her naked skin. The burning in her legs for holding herself spread.

Toweling off, she half expected to find her family awake and waiting for her just outside. But the bedroom was still dark, her husband still asleep.

That helped some, although the guilty thoughts still haunted her. Why did she always go back to AJ? A guy like that didn't have respect for her—for women in general. She wasn't going to be just another notch on his bedpost.

She'd picked her outfit out the night before. She'd left the lingerie on their dresser, and wondered if Max had noticed the pile of expensive lace. It was all new—a matching thong and bra set of rich champagne, nude-colored stockings still in their packaging, a garter belt. She fingered the garter belt, thinking about how Bradley would react if he discovered it. Heat licked between her thighs.

She dressed in the bathroom, reveling in the feel of the soft, expensive lace against her naked skin. She'd always liked lingerie, but putting it on for another man added a whole new level of excitement.

Next came hair and make-up. She didn't overdo it. She was still dressing for work. She wanted to project sexy professionalism, not high-class call girl. Blush, a little mascara, even less eyeliner. She wore lipstick a shade darker than she normally would, but left the fire engine red in the makeup kit. After blowing and brushing out her hair, she coiled it back into the bun that she always wore to work, pinning the stray hair in place, although she left her coppery bangs loose, tucking them back behind her ears.

She checked herself out, and had to admit that she looked good. In her lingerie and makeup, she was a corporate exec's wet dream. The bra was more aggressive than ones she typically wore, a liquid-filled push-up bra that did filthy things to her breasts.

The bedroom was still dark when she finally emerged, but she could sense that Max was awake. She felt his eyes on her, watching her as she dressed. It made her even more excited.

She put on her heels first, more for her husband's enjoyment than anything else. She'd picked out tall black pumps; professional, yet like her bra, more on the aggressive side. Walking in these things for too long wouldn't be practical, but she'd spend most of the day sitting down, and she loved the way they made her butt look.

The black suit was similar to the one she'd worn on her final Friday at IMBARK, only rather than trousers, this one featured a tight pencil skirt that ended just above her knee. The tailored jacket didn't require a blouse, and Katie didn't wear one. Even with the enhanced cleavage, the jacket only hinted at what she had to offer—although she knew from experience that with the right angle, the offer could be quite bold.

"How do I look?" Katie asked when everything was in place.

"Fuckable," Max said. He looked good. He'd settled into a reclined position on his pillows, one arm behind his head, the other hidden beneath the blankets. She could guess what he was doing.

She felt fuckable, that was for sure. She felt fiery as she strolled around the bed, feeling him follow her with his eyes. She took a seat beside him, touching her face. "You're my husband. You *have* to say that."

Max ran his hand up along her stocking-clad leg, under the skirt. When he felt the lace at the tops and touched the clip of the garter, he nodded. "Yes, that's the only reason I said it. Because I'm your husband."

"Think I should go out and see if another man agrees?" She slid her hand under the sheets, finding his cock hard. "Mmm. Think

Bradley Spencer will have the same reaction?"

Max's face lit up. She saw his excitement war with his jealousy, same as always.

Pulling the sheets away, she dropped her mouth to his erection, swirling her tongue around his crown. She tasted the saltiness of his pre-come, drinking it down as she took the full length of his shaft into her mouth. She pumped him three times before drawing back.

Max gasped as she released him from her mouth. He was so hard in her hand.

"What do you think Mr. Spencer would do if I did that?"

"Think you'll find out?" he asked.

"I hope so." She did, although she was still undecided on the matter.

"Whatever happens, I love you," Max said. Katie almost laughed—wasn't that what *she* was supposed to say to *him*?

"I'll see you later tonight, Max."

"Or tomorrow morning."

Katie rolled her eyes. "I'll text you with updates when I can."

****

Katie had no plan beyond choosing an outfit and figuring out how to wear her makeup—and she didn't like it. She was a planner. She went into everything with a strategy. On the way in to work, she wondered why she didn't have one for Bradley Spencer. The easy answer was that she didn't know what she was doing. It had been years since she'd actually seduced someone. Since this game began, she'd always been the one seduced.

But maybe her lack of a plan indicated something deeper. Maybe it was her subconscious saying that she didn't want to do this at all. It was a bad move to get involved with another man. She had

Nadia and John to keep things interesting. Why did she need to introduce an unknown into the equation?

Then she walked into IMBARK and Bradley Spencer was there, looking strapping and fit in his charcoal gray suit, and she decided to let whatever would happen, happen.

"It's good to see you again, Katie." His smile might as well have sparkled.

She squeezed the handle of her briefcase. "You guys causing trouble again?"

Bradley's laugh came easily. "Maybe we were just looking for an excuse to bring you back."

Katie smiled. "That's a costly pickup line. You could have just asked me out."

Bradley tried to play it cool, but Katie saw the surprise before he got it under control. "And you would have said *yes*?"

"I would have thought about it." She was flirting without a net, and it was exhilarating. "So am I back in the little conference room today?"

"Not today. I figured since you were here for just the day, you could set up in my office."

Katie raised an eyebrow. "I see you've got this all planned out."

Bradley's laugh was a touch forced. He ran his gaze over her, lingering at her cleavage, before meeting her playful stare. "You seemed to have planned out a few things, too. Now come on—let me show you my home away from home."

****

Bradley's office was a fairly large one, overlooking a different street than her conference room. For a fleeting moment, she thought wistfully of her view into City Fitness. Then promptly *stopped* thinking that.

Bradley had cleared the opposite side of his desk for her, and already had most of the paperwork she'd need printed out.

"This should get you through most of it. Unfortunately I need to go to a meeting this morning, but you know my staff, and they can help you—probably better than me."

"Thanks, Bradley."

"And please don't leave before I'm out."

"Oh?"

Bradley flashed her a smile. "I plan on firing you. Then taking you out to lunch."

Katie's stomach fluttered at the implications.

"I'll be here."

She blew through her tasks in the first hour and stretched out the rest of the morning writing her report. And drinking coffee. And reading the news on her phone.

Mostly, though, Katie waited. And as she waited, she questioned what the hell she was doing. She'd go to lunch. They'd flirt. They'd drink. She'd suggest that she was more available than most married women. He'd suggest they go check out the rooms at a boutique hotel around the corner. They'd spend the afternoon fucking, and then… And then she'd shower and go home to her family?

On the one hand, the idea of the fling was breathtakingly exciting. To be wanted. To be desired. To be bent over the desk in Bradley's office and fucked. Those were the things that she'd been focused on ever since she knew she'd be returning to IMBARK. But on the other…

She looked around Bradley's office. He had a wall of awards and certifications. A putter and golf ball sat in one corner. And on that desk she'd just imagined being bent over? It was adorned with nautical themed paperweights, weighing down stacks of papers that were meticulously lined up.

As she waited, her anxiety began to eclipse her excitement. She considered just leaving. Of never looking back. Twice, she put on her coat. Twice, she stopped herself, thinking of Bradley's reaction to discovering her garter belt and the way his mouth would drop open when she released her long, red hair from its bun.

She hadn't felt this nervous since the long flight back from Hong Kong, when she didn't know what remained of her marriage.

Just past noon, Bradley popped out, looking annoyed.

"Sorry, sorry." He ground his teeth, clearly angry. "I'm going to be in this thing for the rest of the afternoon. Long-range budget planning—guys can't agree on something three years out."

"People love to talk about the hypotheticals," Katie said.

"Right? This shit's all going to change anyway."

Katie felt his pain. She also felt relieved. "Well, I've got all that I need. Guess we'll have to take a rain check on lunch?"

He looked like someone had just postponed Christmas. Nodding grimly, he said, "Sorry about that."

Katie put on a smile that wasn't entirely forced. "No worries. Not your fault. Good luck in there, Bradley. Call me."

Did she mean that? She wasn't sure.

An important-looking man popped his head in. He glanced at Katie in a way that made her wish that her skirt wasn't so tight and the top showed less skin. Then she was promptly ignored.

"Brad, ready? We're starting again."

"Of course." The guy stood there, waiting for Bradley to follow. It was a strange sight to see, and Katie felt embarrassed for the CFO. "Nice seeing you again, Katie."

Katie packed up her things when Bradley was gone, trying to

figure out if she should feel more relieved, or more frustrated. She could almost hear Nadia admonishing her: *That's your problem, Kates. You overthink how you* should *feel rather than just going with it.*

But that's how she was, and Katie had learned to stop fighting it. She overthought things. She worked through her emotions. There was comfort in that—a sense of control.

On her way out, she swung by the small conference room that she'd called home the last time, sweeping the windows—out of habit, of course.

A table had been set up on the sidewalk outside of the gym, decorated with balloons and a sign advertising some kind of membership promotion. Two people in City Fitness blue polos manned the table, trying to get the attention of passers-by. If ever there was a time to pretend to check it out, now was it.

Not that she had any intention of doing that…

Which was why Katie was puzzled by how she ended up chatting with a bubbly blonde named Lilly at that table five minutes later.

"Hey there, interested in becoming a member?" Lilly had a petite, gymnast's body, and a welcoming smile, despite the chill in the air and the sense of rejection. Katie didn't have the heart to deliver yet another rebuff.

"I'm not really sure. Do you have any locations outside of the city?"

Lilly perked up at the legitimate question. "We do, actually. We've got a facility in Arlington, one just opened in the Tysons area, and there's one in…Bethesda, I think. Where do you live?"

"Closer to Tysons than any of those others."

"Well, aside from the one right here, it's the nicest. State-of-the-art equipment, tons of classes, Olympic-sized lap pool."

Katie was actually more intrigued than she thought she'd be. "How are the yoga classes?"

"Oh, they're great. We have some of the best certified instructors in the area teaching the classes. Most of them have their own studios, but teach a class a week at City Fitness."

Lilly must have detected the genuine interest in Katie's face. She went for the sell. "Sign up today and we'll waive the initiation fee. I'll also make sure to throw in a month's worth of yoga classes."

Katie almost laughed to herself. This was definitely not how she thought she'd be spending her afternoon. It was probably better this way. "I'd have to see the one out in Tysons…"

"Of course." Lilly thought a moment. "Actually, there's a trainer here who splits his time between the two. Why don't you talk to him first?" She lifted her walkie-talkie before Katie could back out. And what Lilly said next froze Katie's blood. "AJ, can you come down here? There's someone who's got a few questions…"

CHAPTER 8

Katie's first instinct was to run. She knew exactly how AJ would interpret this situation and she began crafting an excuse to get out of there before the man showed up at the door—*Oh, I forgot I have a doctor's appointment right now,* or *I really should discuss this with my husband.*

But as quickly as she lost her senses, she got them back. Katie didn't run from challenges, no matter how big they were. In the grand scheme of things, AJ wasn't much of a challenge. She'd weathered a Federal corruption investigation. She'd put CEOs of Fortune 500 companies in their place. Dealing with a jock with the wrong impression of her would be easy.

AJ seemed surprised to see her standing there. His brows went up, even as that insufferable smile stretched across his face.

"Well, well... Decided to check out our facilities after all, huh?" he said.

Lilly looked between them. "You two know each other?"

Hearing the suggestion in her voice was worse than AJ's cockiness—how often did this man *know* the female clientele?

"We've met before," AJ answered without taking his eyes off Katie. "Glad you decided to give us a chance. Come on, let's show you everything we have to offer."

Katie's stomach squirmed. He filled the blue polo shirt out well—nice arms, full chest. When she looked back at his face, though, she blushed.

She found her voice. "Lilly here was telling me that you've got a location out in Tysons Corner?"

"We do. Fact, we've got ourselves members coming out during the work week, then out there on the weekends or evenings." He stepped aside and held the door for her.

Katie looked into the gym, saw the front desk, smelled the universal gym odor of rubber and sweat, and once again thought of running away. Instead, she said, "Such a gentleman." Then stepped inside.

The first part of the tour was a legitimate one. He showed her the front desk, the locker rooms, the basement pool. The weight room—mostly occupied by guys—was on the first floor. They swung by the offices on their way to the cardio room on the second floor. "I'll show you my office if ya like. Nice and private."

Katie rolled her eyes, but watched his sculpted ass as he ducked into the back.

On the second floor, they paused in front of the large windows. Katie glanced across the street, where the offices of IMBARK were. The windows into that building were reflective, but not opaque. He definitely could have seen her just as clearly as she saw him.

"You get a pretty nice view while on the treadmills," AJ said.

"I see that," Katie said. "You spend a lot of time looking out there?"

"When there's something worth looking at." He smiled at her. "So what're you looking for?" After a pause, he added: "In a gym?"

She ignored the obvious retort and answered it like it was a legitimate question. "Mostly the classes."

AJ nodded. "Yoga and Pilates?"

"Pretty much, yeah."

"Lilly tell you our instructors all come from studios around the city?"

"She did."

"That was my idea," he said with a grin. "It's a tricky thing, right? Take you, for example. Before you heard that, what was your impression of our yoga classes?"

"Not good. I mean, not bad, but—"

"Not good. Right? Like a fast food version of yoga. Gym classes are to yoga as McDonalds are to burgers."

Katie's brows went up. "A personal trainer who knows his analogies. I'm impressed."

AJ looked around before winking at her. "Don't go saying that too loud. I've got a rep to protect."

"Of course, of course."

"Come on, let's check out the group exercise rooms."

"Lead on."

As AJ led her up to the third floor, Katie thought about his move to legitimize their yoga class offerings. She didn't want to sound like a snob, but his analogy rang true for her. She always considered the gym to be the source of budget quality classes. Sure, they did well with spin classes, Zumba, or aerobic kickboxing. But there was an art to yoga that she didn't trust to the employees of City Fitness. Pretentious, sure, but she knew that she wasn't alone. And AJ had the awareness to recognize it. Maybe she hadn't given the guy enough credit.

"All classes are up here. We've got ourselves four rooms, plus a open spaces for stretching and working out on your own."

They passed by those open rooms, where a few women were doing planks and crunches on cushioned pads. The room was filled with afternoon light from the street. Katie wasn't sure how she felt about that—exercising in front of the world didn't seem right.

He led them down a corridor, where open doors marked the actual exercise rooms. All were appointed the same way—light wooden floors, mirrors along three of the walls. In one there was a barre, like a ballerina studio. In another, rows of stationery bikes. He led her into the last one at the end and flipped on the lights. Unlike the first she'd seen, this one had no windows.

Her heartbeat picked up a notch as she heard the door close behind her.

"This room is used for Bikram yoga—"

"Hot yoga?"

"Yup. Pilates, too. Course they don't need the heat control."

In the mirror, she watched him turn to a dial by the door and crank it up. Almost immediately, she felt the temperature begin to rise. "What are you doing?"

"Demonstrating the capabilities of City Fitness, of course."

She spoke to his reflection. There was safety in that sense of disembodiment. "That's not necessary. I'm not a huge fan of hot yoga."

"Maybe you just haven't given it a chance," he said. She watched him approach her own reflection, standing frozen in the center of the room in her tight black suit. She could see the way he looked at her, checking her out. Her temperature spiked. She tried blaming it on the room. "Maybe you just need to open up a little."

He slid in behind her. She gasped, then immediately hated herself for it.

"What do you think you're doing?"

He grinned at her through the mirror. "Making sure you don't get these things all sweaty? Or are we done playing games?" His hands went for the buttons of her jacket before she twisted away and turned.

"I'm sorry you got the wrong impression. I thought I was just getting the tour." Her nipples screamed against the rich lace of her bra. Stepping around him, she went for the door. "I'm leaving."

AJ was right behind her, and when she reached for the door, he slammed his palm into it, holding it shut. "I don't think so."

Fear sizzled through her. Fear and something else. "Excuse me, but what do you think you're doing?"

"Cutting to the chase. We both know what you're really looking for." With his arm stiff and straight against the door, she realized how close he was. Their eyes met, his dark and hungry.

"You really think you're hot shit, don't you?"

AJ grinned. "Uh huh."

Before she could marshal a defense, AJ kissed her. She opened her mouth to protest, only to find his tongue pushing past her lips. They were right back there in that alley, making out, hot and heavy, totally consumed with one another.

He took her hands in his and held them above her head, holding her fast. She hated to admit it, but a deep, dark part of her liked the helplessness of the position.

"You know, I've thought about you a lot since that time in New York," he said, releasing her lips for a moment. He kissed along her jaw and into the sensitive spoke behind her ear. She lolled her head to the side, giving him more access. Their fingers entwined—still high and held against the wall above her. "I knew I should have pushed. I knew you wanted it."

When he released her hands, she clutched at his head rather than push him away. She ran her fingers through his hair, holding him close as he kissed down her neck.

Free to let his own hands roam, he made quick work of the buttons on her jacket.

"Damn, girl, I knew you were stacked, but these are fine." He ran his thumb along the top half of the cups, grinning as he discovered her hard nipples.

Katie leaned back against the door. Her grip tightened on his head and neck for support as he ran kisses along her collarbone. Her eyelids drooped. AJ pulled her bra down, baring the tops of her tits. Hot air hit her nipples.

His hands were callused, used to clutching weights. She moaned at the rough touch.

His mouth returned to hers, the weight of him pressing her against the wall. He continued to tweak her nipple, even as he coiled his tongue against hers, coaxing it into action.

He said, "Feel what you do to me?"

Katie reached down between his legs. Finding his erection, thick and large. She'd seen pictures of it—had dreamt about it in the months since—but feeling it in the palm of her hand set her heart racing.

"That's it, baby, squeeze it. You like that, don't you?"

She wanted to tell him *no* and wipe away that smugness. Instead, he stepped back, taking her hand with him, and led her across to the room to the mirror on the opposite wall. She caught their reflection—AJ and the obscene bulge in his pants, Katie with her jacket hanging open, her bra nothing more than a shelf to display her tits.

AJ pulled his shirt off in one fluid motion. He was every bit as sexy as those photos on Nadia's phone had suggested. He wasn't bulky, but he wasn't slim, either. Traps, pecs, biceps, triceps, and wow, those abs; he was a specimen of masculinity. The rich all-over tan added to his beautiful perfection. He turned toward her, leaning against the barre that ran the length of the mirror. The way he grabbed that barre with his hands rolled his shoulders back and pushed his chest out.

"I'll show you mine if you show me yours," he said.

Katie's spine sizzled. She pulled off her jacket, leaving it on the floor behind her. Her fingers shook as she pinched the zipper of her skirt and drew it down her hip. Easing her thumbs into the tight black material, she wiggled free. It joined her jacket on the floor.

AJ whistled, taking in the garter belt and stockings. The matching thong. "Very, very nice, Katie. *Very* nice. Now come over here and suck my cock."

His order struck like a thunderbolt. Any other man would have earned a slap. But with AJ...with AJ, she found herself closing the gap between them and sinking to her knees. Maybe it was the heat of the room. Maybe it was the build-up from earlier in the day, all that anticipation for an illicit afternoon with Bradley that never was.

Whatever it was, as she looked up at him, as she ran her fingers up the smooth material of his track pants, her whole body was on fire. She grasped his waistband and pulled, taking down both pants and white boxer-briefs. Like the rest of his chiseled upper body, his cock was free of hair, making it look even larger as it sprang free.

Katie's mouth fell open. Her chest tightened. Her breathing came shallow. She grasped the thick shaft, unable to circle her fingers around it. It curved up and out, capped with an angry purple head that glistened with pre-cum.

"Go on. Suck it. I know you want to."

She shot a look up at him, rediscovering the will to defy. Only she wouldn't do so through denial. She'd own him a different way.

"Oh, dirty girl," AJ said as Katie ran her tongue down the shaft, pushing it against his stomach, and swirled her tongue around his balls. He was shaved bare there, too, making those heavy orbs all the more tempting. "Suck my balls, baby."

She swallowed them whole, rolling them with her tongue before releasing him. AJ sputtered above her, his head slumped back against the mirror. She smiled, licking back up the shaft, tracing zigzags along the sensitive underside. He may have been the hottest guy she'd ever laid eyes on, but he responded just like any other man. She could work with that.

Taking his cockhead into her mouth, she swirled her tongue around the crown, smiling to herself as she felt him shudder above her. She double-fisted the shaft and took half of it into her mouth before slowly pulling back. Her lips popped off the head with a satisfying smack. She looked up at him with a smile.

"You're enjoying this, aren't you?" he said.

"Not as much as you are." She lapped at him playfully.

AJ smirked, his hands tightening on the barre behind him. "I'm okay with that."

The way he looked at her as she sucked him back into her mouth was thrilling. She maintained eye contact, her greens meeting his dark browns, challenging herself to take as much as she could before gagging. That amounted to less than she wanted to, so she pulled back, drew in a deep breath, and swallowed him into her throat.

His reaction was so satisfying: the open mouth, the groan, the way his whole body flexed—that alone was worth it. She cupped his balls, tugging gently at them as her lips touched the bare root of his member. She retreated before she choked, then struck again. She'd learned to deep-throat with Greg, but Max was big enough to give her plenty of practice.

AJ reached down and released her hair from its bun. She stroked it out of her face, knowing how important the visual was for guys—the way his cock disappeared into her mouth, the way her cheekbones stood out as her cheeks caved with each suck. He licked his lips as he watched, tightness forming in his face. He was close. She sped up, bobbing her head in long strokes from base to crown, throat, tongue, mouth, lips, all working the full sweep of his impressive cock.

His brow crumpled. She saw his teeth clench and grind.

"Yes," he hissed, nostrils flaring.

Faster she worked. Swifter. Her tongue protested as it whipped back and forth. Her jaw was sore. But like a marathon runner, she found that last reserve of energy and sprinted across the finish line.

"Fuck!" AJ groaned. His head snapped back.

Katie was mesmerized by the way the muscles in his neck tightened. Here was a powerful beast, strapped down and struggling for escape. She was the one holding him down. *She* was his mistress.

With one last swirl of her tongue, one last tug on his scrotum, he was there, exploding inside her mouth. She tightened her lips around the pulsing member and swallowed it as quickly as he came.

She released him from her mouth only when he was done and all that swollen manhood started to soften. She sat back on her heels, continuing to pump him with her left hand. Her wedding band caught in the light—a reminder of who she was and who she was married to. What would Max think if he could see her now? Would he be as proud as she was to tame such a wild animal?

"That all you've got?" she said.

As soon as she issued the challenge, she felt his cock twitch and begin to recover. So predictable, she thought.

"You know it's not." He nudged his pants with his toe. "I've got a present in there for us."

Katie knew what it was before he finished the sentence. She reached into the pocket and felt the perforated edge of the condom wrapper, shaking her head with a smile.

"So this what you swung by your office for?" she asked, holding it up. "You were that sure of yourself?"

She stood, amused.

"Was I wrong?"

She tore it open. "Nope."

And just like that, she let it all go. She was going to fuck this cocky son of a bitch, and she was going to love doing it. *That was the idea, right Max?*

She rolled the condom down his once-again-hard length, flashing her eyes as she snapped it into place. AJ met her stare-for-stare, just as amused.

When the condom was set, he took her shoulders and spun her away. She gasped as he bent her over, grabbing the rail along the wall to steady herself. This close to the mirror, she could just barely see his reflection as he moved into position behind her, although she could feel his hands all over her.

"You have an amazing ass," he said. He squeezed her cheeks. "Like a perfect fucking heart."

That felt good to hear. Katie sometimes wished that she had a smaller butt, and felt that she could never get it back to pre-baby shape.

Behind her, AJ skimmed his fingers along her spine and unfastened her bra. He drew his knuckles back down her back, sending jolts of electricity wherever he touched her—shoulder blades, spine, the small of her back.

She didn't need to see him to feel his lusty appraisal of her tight curves. He didn't need to say, *Very nice,* for her to get a thrill. He said it anyway.

"Very nice, Katie." He pushed down on her lower back, forcing her to bend further, to push her ass out more. "Very, very nice."

She caught movement to her right. Her heart constricted. Panic seized her. They'd been caught. Someone had walked in! She shot a glance in that direction only to see herself looking right back. Her reflection.

The panic gave way to a rush just as disorienting. The woman standing there—bent forward, clutching the railing, topless but still dressed in her garter belt, stockings, and thong—couldn't be her. In profile, the curve of AJ's large cock was even more prominent, hooking up like a bow ready to loose an arrow.

She watched that man pull the reflected woman's thong to the side—even as she felt him do it behind her. Her breath caught. She snapped back into herself, into the body of that sexy redhead in the mirror.

For a fleeting moment, she imagined her husband leaning against the back wall, watching from across the room. *This is happening, Max. This is it.*

Then AJ stepped forward, easing his cock into her pussy, and Max vanished in a swell of lust. She clutched the barre harder as AJ slowly sank into her—filling her like no one before him. He was *huge.*

"Slowly," she said tightly. She felt like she was hyperventilating. "Go slowly."

"Not used to taking nine inches, huh? Don't worry, I know what I'm doing."

Katie formed some glib remark about how men always boasted in inches, but couldn't focus enough to actually deliver it. Instead, she dropped her head between her shoulders, her hair falling around her, and moaned into the wooden floor boards.

He felt even bigger than it looked. She loved how Max filled her, but with AJ, she was just so full.

"You're so tight," AJ said. "Look at us. Look how hot we are together."

She shook her hair out of her face, meeting his eyes in the mirror.

The disembodied feeling was back. She watched him touch her in the mirror—running a hand along her back, guiding her hips in time with his thrusts—and while she felt it happening to her, she couldn't sync up the two. Like one was an echo of the other—and neither of them quite real.

AJ didn't just have a large cock. He knew how to use it. He knew exactly how to drive the natural curve of it right against her g-spot, hard and certain. He manhandled her, adjusting his angle, her hips, the spread of her legs. He brought her to the edge of orgasm before her brain had a chance to comprehend the situation, and by then, she was too far gone.

"You know what one of the best features of this room is?" AJ said. He pumped her, building pressure with each thrust—pressure to scream, pressure to explode. "They're all sound proof."

He spanked her ass, sending a wet slap through the room to emphasize his point. Katie yelped. She'd never been spanked before other than this one time with Max that had ended in laughter. With AJ, though, there was an edge. She didn't feel like laughing.

He rubbed the spot where he'd just spanked her, his thumb tracing down the crack of her ass. "Ever taken it here?" he asked.

Katie delivered her response between heavy sighs. "No."

"What's that? I couldn't hear you." He pressed his thumb against her anus. He might as well have touched a match to gunpowder.

For a moment, all that she could focus on was the pressure of his granite hard cock splitting her deep, and the even more intense pressure on her asshole. She went off with a scream.

He withdrew from her as her brain rebooted. After the intensity of the last few moments, she felt empty without him. She didn't need to wait long.

The floor was warm on her back from the Bikram humidity of the room. She focused on that at first, until she felt hands on her thong, dragging it over her thighs.

"A natural redhead," she heard AJ say appreciatively, somewhere above her. "Nice landing strip, although I definitely prefer my sluts bare."

Katie managed to find her voice. She still couldn't get her eyes open. "I'm not one of your sluts."

"That so?" A moment later, she felt him push into her, filling her to capacity with his huge cock. "I have evidence that suggests otherwise."

Katie tried protesting, but like earlier, all she could manage was a moan. The sensation of being so full scrambled everything. With each thrust—"Oh, God!"—with each drive—"Oh, yes!"—his cock grazed her g-spot in a way she'd never felt during penetration. She'd never even played with a dildo this large, and none that had been so perfectly designed.

She arched her back into him, lifting one stocking clad leg over his back, urging him faster.

"You like that, don't you?" he said.

"Yes. Yes!"

"Tell me more, slut. Tell me what you like."

"Harder. Harder," she said. "You feel so good."

"You like a good hard cock, don't you?"

"Yes!"

"Say it," he demanded.

"I like...I like a good...uh...hard...cock..."

He lifted a leg over his shoulder, splitting her open even more. His cock continued to drive home. A second orgasm grew.

He directed her head to the side. "Open your eyes. Look at us."

She did, and there they were, sprawled out on the floor, AJ looming over her, powerful and naked. His body glistened with sweat. His muscles stood out under the exertion of the sex.

He ran a hand up the leg that was on his shoulder, touching the garter straps. "Hot, right?"

She nodded, her response clipped. "Yes." She couldn't seem to breathe deeply enough.

"Look at that slut getting fucked. She loves it." AJ fucked her faster. Planting his free hand beside her, he lifted her off the floor. She hooked her leg further over his shoulder, but she didn't need to worry. She wasn't going anywhere. AJ held her securely.

"Let go, slut. Sound proof, remember?"

Katie nodded, but habits die hard. Her moans came, but she restrained them.

"That's not going to do," AJ said. Keeping his cock buried deep, he held her leg against him as he rose onto his knees.

In the mirror, she saw the whole pornographic scene. She was splayed open, toes pointed out, one foot on the floor, the other behind his neck. Her garter framed the sight of AJ's thick cock—as bare as her pussy lips—penetrating her pussy.

The new angle sent him deeper than ever. She watched him dip again and again into her cunt. His fingers found her clit. Reality unhinged itself.

"Tell me you love my cock," AJ demanded.

"AJ..."

He pressed harder on her clit. Her eyes rolled back into her head. "Tell. Me."

The old, stubborn part of her found a voice. She bared her teeth. "You really...need...that kind of...reassurance?"

Her defiance seemed to spur him on. He jackhammered her, his fingers strumming and slapping her pussy harder than any man she'd been with. She sensed him closing in on his own climax.

"Let go, slut. I want that scream now."

He rammed into her one last time, pressing all his weight on her g-spot. She felt his balls seize up. Felt his shaft swell and pulsate, filling the condom.

That was all she needed. She felt the scream he wanted her to give him. Felt it, and bit down, holding it in as her world blurred in the intensity of the illicit orgasm. She flattened her arms out to either side, stretching her fingers as pleasure tingled out the tips. Her head rocked back until it wouldn't go any further. The world blurred into nothing.

When the climax finally released her, AJ was still there. Still buried deep in her pussy. He'd lowered her to the floor and was studying her—this time directly.

"That concludes my tour of what City Fitness has to offer," he said.

Katie couldn't help laughing. AJ pulled out of her at last, although she remained prone on the floor, energy sapped.

"I see. Such personal attention."

AJ grinned. "We pride ourselves on excellent customer service."

"Is that what they're calling it these days?"

He smiled at her and went on. "Here's what you're going to do.

You're going to go downstairs and shower, because you look like you just had sex with someone in a hot yoga studio—"

She laughed. "Who, me?"

"And then you're going to sign up for a membership. I'm in Virginia on Tuesday and Thursday evenings. I'll make sure I have at least one time slot open."

"What makes you think I'm going to do any of that?"

He ignored her. "I can't wait to see you in your workout clothes. One of the reasons I got into this field was because of my fetish for racer backs."

He stood, careful as he rolled off the condom, and posed for a moment. He was an Adonis, bronzed and molded to masculine perfection. And he was hers if she wanted it.

He pulled on his pants and shirt without bothering to put on his underwear.

"There aren't any classes in here until 5, so take your time. I'll see you next week. It was nice to finally get to know you better, Katie."

And with that, he left her alone.

CHAPTER 9

Katie spent a good long time on the floor of the Bikram room, reflecting on what had just happened. She probably should have felt ashamed at her behavior—at how easily she'd let go with a man she should have been annoyed with.

Instead, all she could do was grin up at the ceiling like an idiot.

She did feel guilt, although it registered like a muted hum in the background. She could easily justify this away. It wasn't like AJ was the first man she'd slept with since Max. And she had full permission to play.

But this felt different than those past encounters—and even the potential one with Bradley. This felt more her own. Felt more selfish. A sexual itch that needed to be scratched.

She picked herself off the floor and went to the mirror. Her body glistened. Her hair was a mess. She'd definitely need a shower.

Her stockings, she was surprised to see, were still in good shape, although uncomfortable in the heat of the room. She touched her pussy, her fingertips lingering on the strip of trimmed auburn curls.

I prefer my sluts bare.

Aloud, she said, "Not going to happen." It felt good to say, even without AJ there.

Quickly dressing, she stuffed her bra and panties into her bag. On her way down to the locker room, she felt like everyone who looked at her knew exactly what had just happened. They looked at her sweaty face and that she was still dressed in a suit, and had to know she'd just fucked a trainer upstairs. Her face was as red as her hair by the time she got into the locker room. She grabbed a towel, hastily stripped and slipped into a shower stall, washing away her shame. Or whatever.

At some point, though, as the water cascaded over her curves and she soaped away the sweat and smell of sex, Katie started smiling—and couldn't stop.

Refreshed and redressed, she tucked everything but her suit and bra into her bag and stepped back into the gym, feeling much better.

She passed by the membership table, where Lilly was signing up a good-looking guy about her age. Like her, he wore a suit—a corporate world warrior looking to stay in his prime. She wondered if Lilly had given him as thorough a tour of the gym as AJ had.

Any guilt at the thought was gone. Instead, it was replace with an exhilarated bewilderment—*did I really just do that?*

Katie took it as a sign that the encounter was probably meant to be a one-time thing. Part of her even liked the idea of a one-night (or one-day) stand. Made it feel even more illicit. She breezed right by the membership desk and headed out the door.

The cold air was good for her. It helped her collect her thoughts and not act heatedly. The more she walked, the more she decided it was a good idea that she hadn't joined the gym. She didn't really have time for them anyway—not between work and Mya—and she still preferred the yoga studios she knew and trusted. And besides, she wasn't going to do something just because AJ told her to.

Then, of course, there was Max. Her husband may have been open to her having a fling, but he also had a history of jealousy. Fantasy was one thing; reality, another.

She thought about the feeling of AJ bending her over and taking her, then repeated that thought: *fantasy was one thing, reality another.*

"Reality is so much better," she said aloud, then laughed.

Her meandering brought her to the storefront of a Lululemon, a fitness and yoga clothing store. Shrugging, she slipped in—more to get out of the cold than anything else, of course—and ended up trying on a couple long yoga tops.

The problem, of course, was that she couldn't try on any of the pants without panties, so she added a few pairs of breathable, athletic thongs to her cart. And of course, she had to try those on. So standing in the dressing room in a thong and a new sports bra, checking out how good her ass looked, she got a wicked idea. Pulling out her phone, she did something she'd never done before—she snapped a racy photo of herself in the mirror, over her shoulder, ass to the camera.

Then, she composed a text to Max.

–Your wife is being naughty.

At first, she attached the photo to it, then decided to just send the message without it. She had no idea who was with him. And besides, it was fun to make him squirm a little as he tried to figure out what she was up to.

–details?

She slipped her phone back into her purse. Let him sweat that one out.

Her trip to the Metro took her by the gym, and one last chance to sign up for a membership. She felt her resolve breaking down as she neared it. She could just imagine how the conversation would go. She thought of herself sitting opposite Lilly, filling out the paperwork:

So AJ made an impression on you, did he? she'd ask.

Katie would stutter a response, which said all but *yes, he fucked me really good.*

Lilly would run down the list of questions, pausing at: *marital status.*

"No, that's not going to happen," Katie said aloud, and kept on walking by the gym.

****

When Katie walked in just shy of five o'clock, Max was in the living room with Mya, working on a jigsaw puzzle. He shot her a confused look, one that said, *You're home so early?*

She shook her head, but couldn't keep the smile from her face.

Later, he cornered her in the kitchen as they cleaned up dinner. "So?"

"So he got held up in some big meeting, and I couldn't really find an excuse to stick around any longer."

"So you were just teasing me..."

"Well, I didn't say that..." She wrapped her arms around Max and pulled him into a long, deep kiss. "No more teasing, Max. Today, your wife was unfaithful."

Max reacted the same way that she did to that word—unfaithful—guilty excitement. That's what this was all about, right? Playing with fire?

"Oh, Katie, I wish I didn't have to work tonight. I really want to hear that story."

Katie had forgotten about tonight's shift. She'd been looking forward to a good seeing to. Despite her afternoon, she was still really horny.

"So skip. Call in sick."

"Katie..."

"You're the boss. Sometimes you get to do that, you know."

He took her shoulders gently, kissing her forehead. "And when was the last time *you* called in sick when you weren't?"

He had a point. They were both too responsible sometimes. But she'd just fucked another man in the middle of a workout room—surely he could make an exception here.

"Fine, but come on." She dragged him toward the stairs to the basement, checking to make sure that Mya was still engrossed in the puzzle.

"Katie?"

Their basement was mostly used as a utility room. Poured concrete floors, unfinished walls, a workout bench on one side, a treadmill that got no use on the other. Katie dragged them over to the washer and dryer, hopping up onto the dryer.

"I just thought that maybe you'd like a taste, before the evidence was gone," she said.

Max looked uncomfortable. "I'm not into...that."

Katie suddenly got what he was thinking and laughed. "Don't worry. He used a condom."

She hiked her skirt up, suddenly self-conscious to be acting this way in front of her husband, despite all they'd been through. Max helped her along, his face lighting up now that he realized she didn't want him to eat another man's come out of her. He stepped up, drawing her down to him for a kiss as he finished pushing her skirt up.

"These are new," he said. "What happened to the thong you left the house in?"

"Gone." Her face was bright as she watched him process the statement. This suddenly wasn't a game, and the enormity of that fact thickened the air around them.

She watched emotion war across his face. Had she made the wrong assumption? Should this game remained just a game—

"Haaa!" Katie moaned as Max pulled her panties off, shoved her legs apart, and dove between her thighs. His tongue zeroed in on her clit and the moistness along her smoothly waxed lips. She threaded her fingers through her hair, cooing at the touch of tongue on pussy.

She reached behind her, cranking the knob to start the dryer beneath and mask her moans. The vibrations were an unexpectedly pleasant side effect.

Max pulled back, looking up at her. "You're so wet," he said.

She hesitated, uncertain what he wanted. Did he want her to tease him more? To reassure him? To tell him she was wet for Max, not her fuck buddy? The dryer rocked beneath her, the heat adding to the eroticism of her exposure. She was wide open for him. She couldn't deny anything.

"It was so hot, baby. I wish you could have seen how bad your wife was."

"You fucked him, didn't you?" Max's voice was practically a growl. "I can taste the condom. You did it."

All that fear and anxiety she had gave way to defiance. This is what he wanted. This is what he'd practically begged her to do. Everything they'd discussed late at night. She still felt that pit in her stomach grow as she formed her reply, but she delivered it with confidence. "Yes, I did. And I loved it."

"You're such a slut," he said.

"That's what you wanted, wasn't it? I sucked his cock. It was so big. I swallowed, too, like a good little slut."

Max was getting off on the taunts. His face went slack, his eyes drooping like he was drunk.

It felt good to be back in control, after an afternoon of being completely out of it. She pulled his head back down between her thighs and draped her legs over his back.

"That's it, baby. Taste me. Taste how naughty I was..."

Max's tongue flew across her pussy, swirling and fluttering at her clit. Whatever reservations he may have had, he was clearly into this.

She braced herself on the back of the dryer, its vibrations lighting up her whole body. Fist in Max's hair, she pumped her pussy into him, feeling everything slide past the point of no return.

She tried forming one last tease at her husband, but it came out as an unintelligible moan. Squeezing his head between her thighs, she tossed her head back and welcomed the rocking embrace of her orgasm. For one jarring moment, she imagined AJ there between her legs. Her body stiffened. She moaned a no. Then came even harder.

Max fell back, crouching on the floor, breathing heavily. He looked up at her—her legs dangled off the spinning dryer, her pussy wet and open.

"So you're serious? You're not fucking with me?"

"I'm an accountant. I'm always serious." She laughed.

Katie pushed up to a sitting position, pulled her skirt back into place, and crossed her legs. Before she could answer seriously, though, Mya shouted from upstairs.

"Daddy! I'm done!"

A moment later, their daughter came stomping down the basement steps. Katie quickly checked her blouse and skirt, making her everything was in place. Max stood, going to the large washbasin to splash water on his face.

Mya's face lit up when she saw Katie. "Mommy! You're home. What are you guys *doing* down here?"

At five years old, Mya wouldn't have a clue, of course, but Max and Katie still stuttered through their answer.

"Laundry."

"Just getting the vacuum."

They looked at each other and cracked up. Max said, "Actually, I need to get ready for work. Come on, let's go get dinner out of the oven."

****

Max left before Katie could tell him about her incident with AJ. She was fine with the delay. She was still trying to wrap her head around it.

She thought of AJ and how different he was from anyone else she'd been with. It wasn't just his confidence—Max had plenty of confidence, especially when they'd first met.

AJ took things a step further. He wasn't just confident that Katie would be attracted to him, he presumed that she'd fuck him that same day. Worse, he'd been right. What did that say about her?

Maybe that was the thing that bothered her the most. Was she that easy? Did Max think so, back in the day? No, of course not. Even five years older than her, Katie knew who drove their relationship. John certainly never presumed as much. Even Greg, for all his faults, had been a gentleman up until the night that was unambiguously about sex.

But AJ just went for it. He was exciting, the way a wild animal was exciting. For a girl from a conservative Connecticut family, at thirty, she was quickly becoming a cliché—and having a good time with it.

As she was powering things down and getting ready for bed, she received an email from Bradley Spencer.

Subject: Sorry about this afternoon

Katie,

You have no idea how much I hate meetings. Sorry they got in the way of our lunch plans. I wanted to show my appreciation for all the hard work you've done for us.

Next week, we're having our annual "winter celebration" (apparently even the word "holiday" is taboo these days), and I wanted to invite you. It's nothing fancy, just a get together at our office. But there's free wine and food, and we know how to have a good time.

We invite all of our consultants, so it wouldn't be weird or anything.

Hope you can come!

Bradley

Bradley Spencer, CPA

Chief Financial Officer, IMBARK

The email made Katie smile. It wasn't hard to read between the lines. He'd missed his opportunity to hook up with her earlier and was manufacturing another.

"We invite all of our consultants, so it wouldn't be weird." That was a telling line—one that suggested that they had something to hide.

Lying back in bed, she considered the email, and then AJ. Would AJ have crafted something so carefully precise? Or would his email been something like, *hey, it's AJ, let's fuck.*

He probably wouldn't have bothered with capitalization, other than for his own name.

That got her laughing, even if it probably wasn't true.

She sent a quick text off to Max, just to mess with him more.

–Bradley Spencer just invited me to his Christmas party next week. Think I should accept?

As she waited, she wondered how she'd respond herself. She liked the guy, and definitely found him attractive. They had good chemistry, that was for sure, and in another life, she could definitely see herself having a fling with him. But AJ had scratched that itch already. She didn't need it any more.

Max's text came in a moment later.

–he's looking for round 2, huh? definitely accept. you can wear that red evening gown.

Katie knew the one. She hadn't worn it in forever—before Mya, certainly—and wondered if she could even fit in it.

She reread the response. *Looking for round 2.* It dawned on her where Max's mind went. He'd assumed that she'd hooked up with Bradley—and why wouldn't he? She'd not mentioned the brash, young personal trainer at all.

It filled her with guilt. She started to compose a correction, but realized that texting wasn't the best medium to communicate a confession like that.

"Later," she said aloud. "I'll tell him later."

But even as she said it, her mind started working through the scenarios. Did she really need to tell him? Did it even matter *who* she was sleeping with, other than the fact that she was?

She kind of liked having a secret—especially a harmless one like AJ. She'd never see the guy again. If she did, she'd tell Max. And in the meantime, she could tease him about this party.

–I know the red dress. But I'll need to go shopping for something to wear under.

She loved the feeling of wearing something sexy and expensive today while at the IMBARK offices, even if Bradley never got to appreciate it. Even better, she loved how excited Max got, knowing what she wore beneath. She'd have to top that...

CHAPTER 10

In the week between the invitation and the actual "Winter Celebration," Katie felt a range of emotions. Guilt was high on the list—even though she'd told Max that she'd slept with another man, she hadn't been entirely truthful about those details. For his part, he didn't pry. He seemed content just knowing that she'd done it, and would likely do it again at the party.

In fact, that was mostly where their conversations ended up.

"So do I get a preview of what Bradley will get next Wednesday?"

"Sure, I can put on my dress again, if you'd like," Katie said coyly.

"And how about what you plan on wearing under?"

"What makes you think he'll see that?"

"Just a hunch."

They had wild, all-out sex through the weekend, every opportunity that they got. Clearly the escalation was a turn-on for Max, but Katie was mature enough to admit that it excited her, too.

That was the other emotion she felt: pure, unadulterated, giddy excitement. Just the possibility that she could so easily fall into bed with another man was intoxicating. Like suddenly the world was truly open to her, and she could have anyone she wanted.

Was this the way AJ felt, every day? Did he look at the women who came into the gym, or into the bar back when he was in New York, and see them as possibilities? The idea of it was so wrong, so different from the way Katie's brain was wired, yet she could see the appeal.

When she met up with Bradley, could she just drag him into the back offices, pull him into his arms, and kiss him? What would AJ do? *WWAJD*. Katie laughed, knowing he'd probably bend her over a conference table, hike up her dress, and take her. Maybe that's what she should do with Bradley?

Merry Christmas. Now fuck me.

She considered calling Nadia and telling her about her fling with AJ. If anyone would understand, it would be Nadia. But Katie had to admit she kind of liked keeping that secret just for herself. There was an illicit excitement to it. And besides, hadn't Max himself said that nothing was forbidden?

Fire, girl. You need to stop playing with that.

****

The Wednesday of the party crept up on her. In the middle of the holiday shopping season, with Christmas less than two weeks away, sex wasn't the only thing on Max and Katie's mind. They took Mya to see Santa Saturday morning. They finally got the lights up on the outside of their house.

Katie braved the mall a couple times to finish off her Christmas shopping list, making sure that Max's parents were covered, along with her own, and all their brothers and sisters, the cousins, nieces and nephews. The older they got and the more their extended family grew, the more complicated the holidays got. This Christmas, they'd be hosting the contingent down at their house, so there was the matter of prepping the place for visitors.

Somewhere in there, Katie managed to pick up a few things for Wednesday night, and she'd already taken Thursday and Friday off to finish any last-minute chores that she may have before the influx of people.

Katie decided to cut out of work early, even though the party wasn't until seven that evening. She was too distracted to get much work done, so decided to book an appointment at a spa. A nice mani-pedi would set her mind at ease.

Nothing's going to happen tonight, she reminded herself. This was all just a big tease for Max. "You're just going to go to the party, have some drinks, and see where the night leads," she told herself. "And you've been speaking out loud to yourself way too much lately."

It felt good to laugh. She'd been so wound up lately, it was nice to release some of that tension. On that note, she decided to add a massage to her spa day. She deserved it.

By seven o'clock, she was in the elevator, nervously riding up to the IMBARK offices dressed in her holiday finest. As she watched herself in the polished chrome of the elevator doors, she thought once again of just calling the whole thing off and going home. Was her dress too much?

Rich crimson, the floor length dress swept down her body like a true evening gown. Spaghetti straps held the tight bodice in place and left her shoulders and the freckled expanse of her upper body bare. It didn't show as much cleavage as some of her other outfits, but it was snug enough to make up for that.

A long slit ran up the front of the silky material of the dress, showing off her stocking-clad legs when she stepped a certain way. Tonight, she'd once again donned her nude stockings, only this time she'd paired them with a blood-red garter belt that matched her bra and thong.

And of course, she brought it all together with a new pair of red high heels that made her feel unbelievably sexy.

The elevator chimed. The murmur of conversation and music spilled through the doors. Too late to turn back now.

"Katie! Wow, you clean up well," said Corey, one of the accountants. He hugged her. Corey was flamboyantly gay, but even he seemed to check her out.

"What? This is just how I look without my glasses."

"Ha! And this is me when I don't wear underwear." He held up his arms, showing off his Euro-cut suit.

Katie looked around, happy to see that everyone had dressed up just as much, if not more, than Katie had. This wasn't some team-building activity that the staff wasn't fully bought into. The people of IMBARK really did decide to throw back.

"Come on, girl, let's get you a drink. You've got some catching up to do. We started partying at five."

"But the invite said seven." Katie said as Corey dragged her into the office.

"Sure, but don't forget, we work here. And we were eager to help the catering crew get started."

"Uh huh."

That said, a drink sounded just about right.

Bradley found her as she was about two-thirds of the way through her first glass of Chardonnay. "Thought I heard your beautiful laugh," he said.

Katie laughed again, unable to help herself. "Well, look at you looking all black tie." She touched the lapel, running her fingers down the dark material.

"Hey, I'm always looking for an excuse to get it out. Don't have nearly as many weddings these days, and the presidential candidates keep forgetting to send me invitations to their inaugural balls."

"Hey, if you ever do get one and need a date, I'm free."

He looked her up and down, smiling. "You realize that I'm going to make it my mission to get an invitation for the next one."

Katie held up her glass. "Happy to motivate, as always."

Time flowed as she mingled through the room, almost always with Bradley at her side. She had more fun than she'd anticipated, and all that anxiety she'd walked in with burned away with the steady conversation and stiff drinks.

The people of IMBARK didn't just know how to have a good time, she realized. They knew how to *drink*. Or thought they did, anyway. At some point, Katie realized that she needed to cut back or she'd end up on the floor. Corey actually did, although he popped right back up and asked for a new drink to replace the one he'd spilled.

Katie laughed. "Oh, boy, things are getting crazy around here."

Bradley smiled. "It's been a really great few months working with you, Katie."

"Well, technically, we've worked together for six days."

"Feels like so much longer though. Next year, I'm going to have to make sure that our bookkeeping is as messy as possible."

"Now that'll just get you more time with the grunts—err, juniors. What you really should just do is keep inviting me to staff parties."

Bradley smiled. "But I don't want to share you with everyone else. How else would I get you into a little conference room, all to myself?"

Katie was suddenly very conscious of her heart beating against her chest. "Well...you could always just ask."

Bradley's face lit up, his lips parting in the barest of gasps. But he didn't ask. Instead he simply said, "That's true..."

It was the decent thing to do, of course. He knew that she was married, and while flirting was acceptable—even the questionable amount they'd done—taking it further seemed to be a line he wasn't going to cross.

Still, Katie was buzzed and horny enough to be disappointed by Bradley's lack of follow-through. Couldn't he see that she was ripe for the taking? She thought of AJ, and how he'd handle this. Were this a City Fitness party, she was positive that she'd be thoroughly fucked by now, probably with the promise of more.

Again, she wondered what would AJ do in this situation. WWA-JD?

"What?" Bradley asked, seeing her quiet laugh.

Katie leaned close. "Meet me in my little conference room in five minutes." She started to leave, then stopped and added, "And make sure no one follows you."

****

Katie stood by the windows, her body silhouetted by the city lights outside. She stared across the street at the gym, lit up with late night fitness buffs. Was AJ working tonight? He'd mentioned traveling to the Virginia location on Tuesdays and Thursdays, but did that mean he had Wednesday nights off?

And then there he was, stepping up next to an attractive woman on the treadmill. The woman nodded at whatever he said, then laughed and touched her hair. Katie rolled her eyes. They were all too easy. But wasn't she?

AJ moved on, working with another runner. As he did, though, he looked out and across the way and did a double take. He definitely saw her standing there, watching him.

He excused himself from the runner, then disappeared into the depths of the gym. She shivered, knowing he was up to something, but uncertain what. A moment later, he appeared on the third floor open workout room, and cut the lights. In his hand was a small white board that he held against the glass.

I GET OFF AT 10. MEET ME OUT FRONT.

She shivered as she read it, but his presumption annoyed her. He wasn't the only player in this game. She didn't have to put everything down whenever AJ crooked his finger at her. As if on cue, the door clicked behind her. She smiled across at AJ, blew him a kiss, and turned to Bradley in the dark.

"So about those reports you wanted," he said. "I couldn't find them. But I brought wine instead."

Katie laughed, seeing that he did indeed have two glasses. "It's a good first step, but I'm afraid I'm going to need more from you."

"Yeah?" He handed her a glass. "Name it."

She took a sip of the wine, fortifying herself—not that she really needed it. She was feeling good—great, even, with her audience of one across the street.

"How about we start here?" Katie said.

She took his head in her hands and drew him down to her, kissing him. It was a sweet kiss—awkward in the way that first kisses were always awkward. Things were still innocent. They could write it off to the alcohol.

Katie didn't want that, and judging from the way Bradley held her against him, neither did he. She pushed her tongue into his mouth, delighted to feel him return it. He tasted like wine, smelled like cologne, and felt nice and hard against her stomach.

Then he pulled back. "Are you sure?"

Katie nodded, feeling small in his arms.

He hesitated, weighing the situation and all its complications. Katie acted before he found his conscience.

"I'm going to make sure we don't renew our contract with IM-BARK next year. Consider this your farewell gift." She kissed him again.

"Now I'm all bittersweet," he said.

Katie mock-pouted. "Let's fix that."

They made out again, her half-seated on the round conference table, him planted between her legs. His hands wandered. His lips left hers to nuzzle her neck. She sighed, giving into the moment. She touched his chest, running her fingers down his stomach.

Pulling herself up onto the table, she reached for his belt, working the clasp. He exhaled slowly, the last of his uncertainly stubbornly hanging on. He didn't stop her, though, and when she drew his fly down, they both held their breath for what came next.

She reached out, running her hand down his nice, hard prick. He was about Max's size, above average and more than enough for her. "Very nice, Bradley."

"Oh, Katie..." He groaned as she stroked it, drawing a bead of pre-come out the tip.

"Is this what you hoped would happen tonight?" she asked, pulling him closer. "When you invited me, were you hoping we'd end up back here, alone in our conference room?"

She felt his answer in the pulse of his cock, but she wanted to hear him say it. She squeezed him. "Well?"

"No," he said. "Not hoped, anyway."

"But fantasized?" She stroked him, enjoying the power her touch gave her.

"Yeah."

"I like being your fantasy."

Pushing the spaghetti straps off her shoulders, she shimmied out of her crimson dress, letting it pool on the floor. "Do I meet your expectations?"

Bradley took in her red lingerie, her garter belt, her stockings, with his eyes wide, mouth agape, nostrils flaring. He nodded at her question.

Katie reached into her clutch and pulled out a condom.

Bradley groaned.

Someone passed by the door behind him, a woman's giggle piercing the door. Bradley froze. Fear and excitement spiked through Katie. This was so wrong. On one side, the threat of discovery. On the other, the entire world, including a man who she hoped was still watching.

"You want it?" she said, offering him the condom.

Bradley struggled for about a millisecond longer, than grabbed it. Running her thumbs into her g-string, she peeled them off and hopped back up onto the table.

In the dim light, Bradley caught a glimpse of her sex, swearing under his breath.

"You like it?" Katie asked. Feeling naughty, she ran her fingers down her landing strip and across her mound, moaning. "I love waxing it. Makes sex so much better."

Bradley's hand shook as he tore open the condom and rolled it on. Katie made it harder for him by pushing two fingers into her pussy and rubbing her clit with her thumb. He didn't want to look away.

At last, he got the latex sheath in place and stepped forward. Katie took his cock in her hand and guided it into place, rubbing the tip along her wet mound.

He sawed along her smooth channel one, two, three times, before readjusting. He placed his cockhead against her pussy and pushed home.

Katie bit her lip, stifling a moan as Bradley Spencer entered her, filling her with his hard, thick shaft. It felt different than Max. Different than AJ. Different than John, or Greg, or any of her past lovers. Every cock was unique—and every cock was available to her. Every cock she wanted, she could have.

It was a slut's epiphany. One that people like Nadia and AJ have been enjoying for years.

Katie wrapped her legs around Bradley's back, pulling him into her harder. She lay back on her elbows. Her hair spilled out behind her. He reached out, squeezing her tits through her bra as he fucked her. The table groaned. Neither of them cared. He yanked her bra down, her tits spilling out over the top of the red lace.

"I've dreamed about these," he said.

"Then suck them," Katie replied, once again feeling the surge of command. She pushed back to more of a sitting position, and Bradley leaned down to suckle her nipples. "Harder," she said. "Don't worry about hurting me."

It wasn't a thing that she normally said—not to Max, not to anyone. But in the moment, she wanted to feel a little pain. She wanted to be punished for what she was doing.

She bit harder on her lip, her nostrils flaring as pain seared through her. Bradley grazed his teeth along her erect nub, immediately following it up with a gentler lick. Then hard again, the cycle short-circuiting her brain.

And the whole time, he fucked her, his strange cock pumping in and out of her juicy sex.

Her head lolled back. She looked out the windows, the world upside down. She reoriented herself, seeking the dark exercise room that AJ had been in. The world dropped off in floors and floors of dark glass. She caught movement in one. The exercise room? Or another, higher up? Was AJ watching? Did this make him jealous?

"Oh, Katie...you feel so...good..." Bradley was close. The words came out pressurized. He clutched her hips and fucked her in short, rapid jerks. She reached between her legs, zeroing in on her clit, but she was already there. She was already keyed up and ready to launch.

Where was AJ? She hoped he was watching. She hoped he couldn't contain himself, finding a dark spot to hide and rub himself as he watched her slut it up for another man.

It was that image that propelled her into orbit. Bradley clamped his mouth over hers to silence her moans, kissing her fervently as he rammed home. She felt his body seize up. A second later, his cock went off inside her, filling the condom with his hot seed.

Bradley lay on top of her for the longest time, breathing heavily. He was still in his suit, only his pants were down around his ankles. Her mind was already working through the next few moments. There was an office full of people out there who could never know about what she'd just done.

No, not just the logistics of escape. The logistics of Bradley. They'd get cleaned up. Leave the room separately. Pretend like nothing had happened. He'd tell her that he wanted to see her again...

Bradley pulled out of her, eyes still closed as he took in a deep, steadying breath. He was a good guy. He deserved more than to be used as a prop to make the asshole across the street jealous. And that's exactly what she'd just done to him—she'd used him.

Something gnawed deep within her, but she pushed it aside, forcing lightness into her voice. "How was that as a parting gift?"

Bradley laughed before realizing the implication in her question. This was it. This would be the last time they saw one another—professionally or otherwise. It nearly broke her heart to watch him accept it. He was gracious enough not to protest.

"Best I'll probably ever have." He zipped up. "You were amazing."

"So were you." It wasn't a lie.

"Want me to leave first?" he said.

Katie nodded.

"Goodbye, Katie." He smiled at her one last time before closing the door behind him. She straightened her bra and pulled her thong back on, but didn't immediately put on her dress. Instead, she went to the window and looked out, scanning the windows of City Fitness. Most of the lights were off. The gym had closed. And AJ was nowhere to be seen.

CHAPTER 11

After what she'd just done, Katie welcomed the night air, stepping out into it without bothering to button up her long wool coat. She'd made an abbreviated departure, which was easy since she didn't really know many of the IMBARK folks, and they were all shit-faced anyway. Her first goal was to secure herself some cigarettes.

Katie wasn't a smoker. She wasn't even a social smoker. But sometimes, she needed a little nicotine to calm her. And when she'd just used a good and decent man for sex, then told him to take a hike? Well, that qualified as one of those times.

The 7-Eleven was still open, smelling like stale coffee and newspaper. She avoided eye contact with the clerk as she ordered a pack of Camel Lights, then hated herself for feeling that shame. She was thirty years old. She could buy cigarettes.

Outside again, she lit up, sucking down the acrid smoke, and instantly felt better. She was able to look back on the last couple hours with the detachment of an observer. She'd had sex with a client. She'd had sex with him and felt terrible for doing it. Why?

She catalogued her thoughts and emotions. It wasn't because she was married. She'd slept with other men before—including one just last week. It wasn't because she was worried that Max would hate her. If anything, he was probably home right now, excited at the prospect of it.

When she'd slept with other men, they'd all been in on "the game." Greg and John came with wives just as kinky as them. AJ was a man-whore. But Bradley was a good guy who she'd played. Sure, she'd been attracted to him, but in the end, she couldn't shake that feeling that she'd used him for…for who? Not Max. How much had she thought about Max while she was up there?

Katie stubbed out the cigarette, and said, "AJ."

As if summoned, he pulled up beside her in his burnt orange Camaro.

"Hey, girl, looking good."

Katie felt giddy at the sight of him, despite herself. "Of course you drive a Camaro," she said.

He revved the engine. "Get in. I'll give you a lift."

"I don't think so."

A car behind him blared its horn. AJ in turn laid on his own. "Move along, asshole," he shouted out the opposite window.

Katie covered her mouth and laughed.

"See what you're doing? You're literally causing a traffic jam." AJ chuckled. "Now come on. Metro sucks this time of night, and you look too good to ride it anyway."

Katie looked up and down the street, anticipation crackling through her. "You promise you'll take me where I want to go?"

"Scout's honor."

He leaned across and opened the door. She slid in to the bucket seat and pulled the door shut. "You were a Boy Scout?"

"Fuck no." And with that, he gunned it.

****

"Didn't know you smoked," AJ said as he navigated them out of the city.

"You don't know much about me."

"I know that you're more complicated than I thought. You wanna appear calculated and in control, but there's this side of you wanting to just fucking let loose."

"So is that why I smoke?"

"Yup." They pulled up to a red light—the last before the bridge into Virginia. He turned to her, looking mischievous in the low light. "That's also why you fuck men in front of windows."

"So you saw?" Her face went hot.

"I watched," he said. Her heartbeat skipped.

"You get all jealous?"

"Do I look like the kind of guy who gets jealous?"

"Maybe. With the right girl," she said.

"And you think you're the right girl?" The light turned green. He accelerated fast enough that the tires squealed.

It pushed Katie back into the scalloped seat. She smiled to herself, figuring that was as much of a win as she'd get.

Katie looked around her. She hadn't been in a true sports car in years—not since Max had traded in his Mustang for a Camry.

In a way, that was the natural progression of things. Sports cars to sedans. City living to the suburbs. Many women to one. She looked at AJ, one hand on the stick shift, the other perched on the top of the leather-wrapped wheel. Would he make those transitions one day? Would he meet the right girl?

For now, though, he was the kind of guy who picked up married women because he didn't give a damn about *long-term*.

"So did you like watching?" Katie asked.

AJ thumbed his nose, glancing quickly at her. "Was pretty hot."

She knew what she was going to do next, and it was crazy even to consider. She was an educated professional. A wife and mother. She was on the PTA!

And despite all that, she found herself unbuckling her seat belt so she could shimmy out of her dress. Everything about the situation was dangerous—the speeding car, the risk of exposure, the cocky young man that she barely knew. It's what made it all so irresistible.

"What are you doing?" AJ asked. The uncertainty in his voice— gone in a flash—was thrilling.

"Giving you a closer look."

AJ scanned her when he could. "Red underwear. Nice."

"'Tis the season," Katie said. She practically giggled as she unfastened it—not that she was a giggler.

"You've got some really nice tits, baby. I bet you like touching them."

Katie scooped the soft swells into her hands, squeezing them. She circled her nipples with her thumbs, but only once. She was so sensitive. She realized that her body was so tightly wound that she was about to come completely unraveled.

"Take the panties off. Don't leave a guy hanging."

She looked around. There were cars, but no one immediately next to them. And besides, she'd gone this far. Might as well finish it. Lifting her hips, she slid them off quickly. The leather felt cool on her bare sex.

AJ slid his hand from the gear shift to her thigh, stroking the lacy band at the top of her stocking. He ran his fingers across the clip of the garter.

His hand moved higher, inching into the hot press of her thighs.

Katie held her breath, stifling a moan as his touch neared her pussy.

When he touched her landing strip, he frowned. "Thought you knew what I liked."

Katie smiled, nibbling on her lower lip. "Oh, I do."

"Little defiance, huh?" He pushed his fingers against her clit. Katie gasped. "I'm going to have to punish you for that."

"Oh yeah?" she asked. A tiny voice in her head protested at how wrong this was even before she acted. Lifting her legs, she hooked the heel of her right foot into the A/C vent and opened her legs. "Feels good enough to me," she said.

Stripped down to her red garter belt, stockings, and heels, she played with her pussy as the world outside flew by. Did any of the cars they passed have a clue what was going on inside AJ's sleek Camaro?

"Ever given road head?" AJ asked.

She shook her head, watching as he reached into his lap and unzipped his jeans. The balance of power inside the car shifted in subtle ways, swinging back towards AJ. Katie glanced at the highway, racing by at seventy miles per hour. This was dangerous—stupid, so many things. Yet when he fished out his cock, she licked her lips, already tasting it in her mouth.

"Go on, you know you want to."

She hated that he was right.

But he was right.

Twisting over the shifter, she worked open the catch of his belt. She glared up at him, and he met it with an insufferable wink. He put a hand on the back of her head and pushed her into his lap. She stiffened, fighting it for only a moment before taking him into her mouth.

"Mmm, yeah, baby. God, your tongue feels good."

She swirled the top half with her tongue, stroking downward

with her lips until he hit the back of her throat. Slowly, she eased back off, releasing him from her mouth with a pop.

"Dangerous, isn't it?" he said. He pushed her hair out of her face, over one shoulder. "I want to watch those pretty lips wrapped around my cock. Now let's get back to work."

She almost refused. Almost. But the rumble of the engine and that exhilarating feeling of speeding through space made this whole experience so hot. So irresistible.

She went back to him, wrapping her hand around the hairless base, jacking him in time with her lips. He gasped over her, threading his free hand into her thick, copper hair. She sucked harder, cheeks hollowing around his shaft. He groaned—pressed down on the gas, pushing the car faster. She could feel it lurch. Could feel it fly. She bobbed faster—out of fear, out of excitement.

"Play with yourself," he said. She ignored him the first time, focusing on the blowjob. "Touch your pussy. Do it."

Compelled, she snaked her free hand between her legs, rubbing her fingers across her slick sex. Zeroing in on her clit with her middle finger, she moaned, sought to pull her head up to breathe. AJ held her fast, his hand tightening in her hair, keeping his cock lodged in her mouth. She moaned harder, sending tremors down his shaft.

"Oh, Jesus, babe. Keep doing that!"

The car sped up, faster and faster. Katie sucked him like her life depended on it—in some way, it did. The only way to get off this ride was to get AJ off, so she used all her tricks. She licked, she hummed, she teased him with the entrance to her throat. Frothy saliva drooled down his balls, filling the cab with the wet *fap fap* as she jacked him.

"Oh, fuck. Damn, you know how to suck...cock!" He stroked her hair back, encouraging her to bounce her head in his lap. He pushed his hips up, her head down, and suddenly he was inside her throat.

She choked. Tried to pull up. His hand formed a fist in her hair.

He was close. She could feel it in his tightening grip on her hair. That hurt, but she liked it. She welcomed the pain.

"That's it. Keep sucking. Keep that shit up!"

He pressed on the gas. How fast were they going? Adrenaline coursed through her, wild and out of control. She pulled back, focusing on the top half of his cock in rapid, cork-screwing lunges. This was her finisher, and she needed to finish before they ended in a fireball streaking down the road. She sucked as hard as she could, working his glans until her tongue cramped. Around and around she went, dizzyingly fast.

AJ grunted. He was close. So close. She moaned, wanting to taste him. Craving his come. She moaned again out of desperation—her last gasp before she wouldn't be able to take it any longer.

It was enough.

AJ's hand cranked down in her hair one last time, drawing a yelp. "Oh, oh! Here it comes! Prepare to swallow!"

She latched her lips around his shaft, drew back until all she held in her mouth was his head, and welcomed the viscous eruption. It felt like he came forever, but Katie proudly swallowed it all.

She popped up and wiped her mouth, smiling proudly at AJ. "That was good," he said. "That was *very* good." He looked glanced past her, out the window on her side. "And for the second time tonight, looks like you've got an audience."

Horror seized her even before she looked. There, matching their break-neck speed, was a white Escalade. Sitting in the front was a beefy-looking black guy with a smile about as wide as his oversized SUV. She covered her breasts and crossed her legs, feeling exposed.

The guy clapped his hands, mouthed a *thank you*, and dropped speed. AJ's Camaro shot away.

Katie's face lit up. AJ laughed. "Guess you gave yet another guy a nice little show."

He took the exit off the highway, and for the first time, Katie got a sense of their surroundings. Gone were the suburbs of Northern Virginia. They'd traveled farther out than she'd realized. The exit they took was onto a lonely road, flanked by rolling farmlands.

"Where are we?"

"Fuck if I know. Virginia? Amazing how rural it can get, so quickly."

Whatever road they were on was a winding one. The stars were clear this far out, lighting up the sky like fireflies.

"Where are we going?"

"There was a sign for a motel back on the highway, and I don't know about you, but I seriously need to fuck."

CHAPTER 12

Katie buried her face in the pillow, her moans more growls than cries. She raised her ass higher, changing the angle of the cock pounding her from behind. So good. So full...

She turned her head enough to breathe, her red hair spilling across her face, sticky with sweat.

"Ah! Ah! Ngh!" She still wore the stockings and garter belt, but the rest of her clothes were a mess across the floor.

"You like that? This what you want?"

"Yes," she moaned. "Fuck me. Oh, please fuck me!!" Her voice cracked as she fought to control her volume.

"Yeah? You want it harder?"

"Yes," she whispered.

"Deeper?"

"Uhh, yes..." God, he felt huge inside her. "So good..."

He pulled on her garter straps, tugging them like the reins of a horse. "Did he spank you? Your ass is red."

"Yes..." He'd called her a naughty slut, she remembered. Said that she deserved it.

Katie looked back at her husband, whose face was twisted in the pain of near orgasm. She had no idea what time it was. Late. But Max had been up, waiting to reclaim her.

"You're so wet, baby," Max said. "You sure he had a condom on?"

"He did," she said. AJ had wanted to. He'd even nearly convinced her, back there in the motel. They'd been all over each other. He'd thrown her onto the bed and pounced. If he hadn't mentioned how he'd just been tested—how he was clean—she would have let him. Oh, the irony.

"I think *you* wish he hadn't," Max said. He pounded her harder, determined to make her his again.

Reclamation sex. They hadn't had it since she'd gone off with Greg so long ago, and Katie forgot how good it could be. She wasn't always for rough sex, but after doing it with two other guys that night, she needed to feel her husband take her.

Three guys in one night! She still couldn't wrap her head around it. The shame of it was crushing, and yet every time she thought about what she'd done, she buzzed.

"You're thinking about him now, aren't you? About your accountant boyfriend."

"No," she intended to say. All that managed to emerge was a garbled protest. Max understood. Or thought he did.

"Sorry. Not boyfriend. Fuck buddy."

Katie's stomach twisted up. Thinking of AJ and his fine and fit body as her *fuck buddy* was a tempting thought. But Max didn't know about him, and she wasn't sure how to break it to him now.

"Just fuck me, Max. Just...fuck me."

Her husband did as she asked, tightening his grip on her hips as he took her from behind. He felt so thick inside her, nice and big, his balls clapping against her swollen sex with each thrust.

"Come, Max. Come inside me. I want to feel it." She lifted her ass higher, letting him take her—take her like AJ had earlier that night. Her breath caught. "Reclaim me. Reclaim your wife."

It was too much for Max. He lasted a couple strokes longer, then exploded inside her. Despite all the sex she'd had in the past day, she'd been denied that intense feeling of man's heat flooding her. With it, she let everything go, giving in to the purity of her orgasm.

Max rolled off her. Katie slumped onto her side. Her body was sore. She'd been moving from encounter to encounter non-stop since she'd left—physically as well as mentally—that everything finally overwhelmed her.

Max's voice drifted to her through a fog. "So you have fun tonight?"

"Too much," she said.

This is the part where she confessed to being with two guys—where she told him that it wasn't just Bradley that she'd been with, but the bartender from New York. And it hadn't just been tonight.

She felt the weight of the confession on her chest. "Max...I was... so bad..."

As Max's arms folded around her, pulling her into a warm snuggle, she nearly sobbed. How could she have kept her encounter at the gym last week from him? It went against everything she believed in. Where was the woman who wouldn't do anything to risk her family?

"I love you so much," Max mumbled. He was falling asleep!

"Max, I need to tell you something..." Her fear was practically palpable, but this had to be done.

"What's that, honey?" He was barely awake. She lifted her head from him and looked down at his peaceful face. His eyes were closed.

His breathing slow.

I was with two men tonight, she thought, not said. "I'll tell you in the morning."

He didn't even respond. He was asleep.

****

Katie dreamed of the night before. She dreamed about the way AJ had fucked—she was on her back and he stood beside the bed, one of her legs over his shoulder, the wicked curve of his cock pummeling her g-spot.

In her dream, though, things got wilder. Bradley was there, too, sitting on the edge of the bed, stroking his cock. She turned, took him into her mouth, blowing him as AJ kept on fucking her. In her dream, it felt so natural. And then there was Max, watching from the door of the motel room, eyes riveted. That had been the hottest thing of all.

"That's it, baby, show them how good you are," the dream Max said. "Fuck them good, then I'll fuck you."

Katie woke with an orgasm, her fingers dancing between her thighs, circling her clit. She was alone, thank goodness, although she still felt the heat of embarrassment.

In those first few moments, as the dream faded and reality returned, she could almost pretend that last night had never happened.

But it had, and with that the realization that it was time to come clean. No more excuses. No more delays.

Well, maybe a shower first. She'd taken one back in the motel before coming home to Max, but she was feeling extra dirty this morning—and it wasn't just from the reclamation sex.

Katie went over her plan under the hiss of the shower. She actually hadn't told any lies yet, just omissions. Max knew about both of her encounters, last week's and last night's. She'd been honest with him about everything but the guy involved.

Not that that gave her any comfort. She'd still omitted the truth. She'd still carried on with AJ and not told Max a thing about it.

But it would be worse to keep on going without him knowing about it. Communication was key to a successful marriage, and she hadn't been holding up her end of the deal very well lately.

Fresh from her shower and dressed in a pair of jeans and a nice, flowy top, she was comfortable. She could do this.

First thing she smelled was coffee—proof that there was a God. Second, bacon. Max had been busy while she slept.

"Good morning, sleepy head," Max said. Mya was sitting at her place at the table, polishing off a syrup-laden stack of pancakes.

"Morning, Mommy!"

Katie nearly burst out crying. How could she even think about risking this scene? How could she be so stupid?

"Morning, you two. Smells yummy."

Max gave her a meaningful look, one that said, *It's okay, relax.* He had no idea.

"Sit down. Your plate's warming in the oven."

"You should think about a career in the service industry," Katie said.

"I should, shouldn't I? Think I'd do well?"

Katie laughed, despite the stilted joke. It felt good to share that with him.

"Speaking of, you'll get a kick out of this. You'll never guess who Nadia just hired to work bar at Callahan's."

Katie's heart clutched, although she didn't fully understand why. "Who?"

"Your friend, AJ."

That was why.

Katie's eyes went wide. Her body froze. She had no idea how to handle this news, so she just stared.

"Maybe you should pop over there for a drink some time?" he said.

It was meant to be a joke, but Katie felt like vomiting.

"What's wrong, Kates?" Max asked, concerned. "I can fire him if you'd like."

Katie looked at Mya, who was blissfully unaware of the enormity of the situation. She slid off her chair, grabbed her plate, and carried it to the sink. "I'm going to watch my shows now."

And off she went.

"Max, I slept with him."

She saw the same frozen shock on his face that she'd just felt. He didn't blink. He didn't move. He looked like she'd just punched him in the stomach.

"I should have told you. I don't even know why I didn't. It just kind of happened, and...I should have told you." She ended looking at her hands, twisting them together, her wedding ring winking up at her.

Max took a deep breath, releasing it slowly. Katie peered up at him. There were so few things that could freak this man out, and she'd successfully freaked him out regardless. He spread his fingers out wide on the kitchen counter, his mind working through all of the implications.

"Say something, hon. Talk to me."

He glanced up sharply, as though surprised to see her there. She readied herself for the yelling—although Max didn't do that. She braced for disaster. Max opened his mouth once, started to speak, then stopped again.

Katie wrung her hands together, wanting to rush to him but unable to move.

When at last he spoke, she couldn't read him at all. That alone was frightening enough. "You slept with him…when?"

Katie flinched. "Last night…and last week, too?" Her voice rose at the end, turning the touchy confession into an uncertainty.

Max released a monstrous sigh. He repeated her answer, feeling its weight. "Last week."

"You know how I told you I'd been bad last week? Well, it wasn't with Bradley…"

Max nodded, but only appeared to half listen. "So back in New York last year, you really did just kiss him."

"Yeah." Then Katie realized where his mind had gone. "Oh, Max, yes, all we did was kiss back then. You've got to believe me—"

Max looked like a man who'd just woken from a long, hard sleep. He blinked, took a steadying breath, and was himself again. "I believe you." His chuckle was borderline hysterical. "Gave me a scare there."

His fear underscored to Katie that as much as he thought he wanted her to be crazy, he didn't really want it.

Katie moved into his lap, pulling him into an intense hug. "I shouldn't have teased you about that. Nothing happened then."

"But something happened last week," Max said.

For one fleeting moment, she felt the flicker of fear. The real confession was back. She may not have harbored a year-long secret, but did that make it any less a secret?

Then Max kissed her. It was a soft kiss—at first, anyway—the perfect kiss for the moment. He held her, nuzzling her nose, his lips the first fit to her own. When he pushed his tongue into her mouth, she welcomed the sensation of being overpowered.

Pulling back, he looked her in the eye. "You're so sexy."

Katie blinked, unable to process his reaction. These numbers didn't add up. "What? I don't understand. You're...you're not upset?"

"No, I am. But it's not that simple." He sucked air in through his clenched teeth. "I'm a little upset that you didn't tell me when it happened, but in a fucked up kind of way, it makes it hotter that you didn't."

"Still...not following."

"Did I ever tell you my concept behind The Katherine?"

"An exclusive speakeasy for hipsters?" Katie dared to smirk, and received one from Max in return.

"Not exactly. I wanted to create a place that gave everyone a taste of something forbidden. When people come through those doors, for an instant, they can pretend they're living in a time when just the act of drinking felt illicit."

"And on top of that, you serve drinks mixed with absinthe, which people still think is illegal," Katie said, starting to get it.

"Right. I think that part of me wanted you to experience that idea of the forbidden. It's exciting to think that my wife and my better half could be out there, being so bad."

"But then Hong Kong happened," Katie said.

"It did." Max laughed nervously. "But I guess it didn't scare me enough."

"Want to know what I honestly think?" Katie asked.

"Always," Max said.

"I think that it's just as much about you as it is about me. The forbidden thing, I mean."

This felt different than writing her actions off to Max's fantasy. She knew her role in this rocky chapter in their life and accepted responsibility for it. This was more mutual. Suddenly—finally—they were in this together.

"Yeah, it is. And I did tell you that nothing was forbidden."

He was giving her an out, but she refused to take it. "That doesn't make it right. I know better than anyone that there are still boundaries. Maintaining trust is one of those boundaries."

Max didn't argue. He nodded. "Look, I need to work today, but we're going to continue this conversation later."

Katie nodded. Definitely.

"And…" His smile diffused a lot of the tension she was feeling, but not all. "If you want to start rebuilding any trust we may have lost, I expect to hear all the dirty little details from last night."

****

Max had to work later that afternoon, so the big reveal would have to wait. In a way, Katie was grateful. She'd be able to plan it out and strategize the best way to go about it.

The other thing that the alone time let her do was think about Bradley once again. She'd wronged the guy. In the cold light of a new day, she saw it plainly. She could tell herself that he shouldn't have expected more, but that was the logical accountant side of her brain rationalizing. The other side of her kind of hated herself for using him like that. It even hated that she'd done it to AJ, although he was a little easier to write-off—especially when he texted her around five o'clock with a booty call.

–hey. it's aj. you free tonight?

It made her laugh, but she texted him back a big, fat NO. He took the hint. No other texts followed.

Katie reflected on how far she and Max had come in the last couple years. Back then, she never would have even fantasized about being with three men in the same night. The idea would have shocked her—maybe even disgusted her. So what had changed?

"I'm turning into Chloe." She finally—*finally*—put voice to the thing that had been troubling her since this whole thing had started up again after Hong Kong. She hated thinking it, so she didn't. Saying it forced it into the open.

She was turning into Chloe. She felt a strange sensation of catharsis, despite the horrible implications that came with a statement like that. She'd held such disdain for the woman from the moment her true nature had been revealed, but how different were Katie's actions? She recalled a conversation she'd had with Max a few months ago.

Do you realize that she had no respect for her husband? She told me as much. She told me that she had the life: she could fuck around with whoever, whenever, without limit, and could go home to her millionaire husband, who'd support her no matter what. She's awful.

Minus the millionaire part, how was she behaving any differently?

Katie was jarred out of her thoughts by the doorbell ringing. It was just after seven. Uncertain who'd be visiting unannounced, she opened the door to John and Nadia.

"Hey. What're you two doing here?"

"Hey there, kid," John said with that disarming way of his. One look at her friends and Katie knew that they knew about last night.

Nadia said, "We're not the one with the real surprises, so I've heard."

Katie blushed. "Come on in."

Mya came out of the kitchen. "Auntie Nadie! Uncle John!"

"Hey, kiddo," John said. He went down onto a knee and wrapping Mya up into his arms. "We're here to babysit as your mom and dad go out on a date."

"Yay!" Mya said. Katie looked at Nadia for clarity.

"Come on, let's go find you some prettier things to wear. I'll explain."

"So you've talked to Max?" Katie asked. They made their way upstairs.

"Uh huh. So you and AJ? I should be upset at you. You were holding out on me!"

"I'm sorry. It just kind of happened."

Nadia smirked. "I bet it did."

Katie slumped onto her bed. "I don't know how you do this."

"Do what?" Nadia started pulling things out of Katie's wardrobe, laying out a few possible outfits for the night.

"I think I'm turning into Chloe."

Nadia stopped what she was doing and looked sharply at Katie. "Chloe, as in I'm Going to Steal Your Husband and Ruin Your Life Chloe?"

Katie shrugged. "I should have told him, Nadia. I slept with AJ last week, and again last night, and I *should have told Max*. But I didn't, because I was being a selfish bitch. I was focused on my own pleasure over anyone else's—"

"But you did tell him," Nadia said. She'd taken a seat next to Katie, who hadn't noticed until she felt Nadia's arm around her. "And, I mean, it's not like we're strangers to this lifestyle."

Katie sighed, shutting her eyes. "No, we're not. But that just makes it worse. I know Max. He's not as confident as he pretends to be. I've seen how bad he can get. Yet I gambled anyway. I *am* Chloe."

"That mean I need to watch out for you and John?" Nadia forced a laugh, breathing levity back into the room. "Look, if you're a Chloe, then so am I. But it's not that simple. You've overcomplicated this, and we all know that sex is already complicated enough."

Katie laughed with her. It felt good, if a little false. "I'm not sure why I'm taking advice from you."

"Oh, fuck you," Nadia laughed. "But yeah, you're right. This sounds like a conversation between you and Max."

"So what's the plan tonight, anyway?"

"Well, you're going out tonight. I've never seen Max so eager to get you alone. John and I figured we'd help that along. So here, let me help you pick something fucking awesome to wear."

Katie felt like this was a first date. She couldn't seem to slow her heart down no matter how much yoga breathing she practiced. The evening didn't feel like a short-and-tight kind of night, so she chose a more modest dress—one that reached her knees and covered her arms and shoulders. Matched with a pair of brown, slouchy boots, she looked casually sexy.

"Approve?" Katie asked, doing a spin for Nadia.

"It's decent."

Katie hugged both Nadia and John, thankful to have them in her life. She wasn't the type to have many friends, and she hated leaning on the few that she had, but she was grateful now.

"Have fun," John said.

"A lot of fun," Nadia added.

And she was off, cabbing into the city as John and Nadia put Mya down for the night.

CHAPTER 13

Starlight Lounge was her husband's first shot at something more up-scale than the Irish pubs he operated. It was clean, polished, pricy—and wildly popular because of those things. Katie always got a kick out of it whenever she visited, largely because it was her idea. Five years ago, when she suggested he open it, this was the kind of bar she and her twenty-something friends frequented. If Max was going to be successful in DC, he needed a place like this on his portfolio.

She scanned the sparse crowd from the doorframe, surprised to see how empty it was for a Saturday night. It was early, but even still she didn't expect so many empty tables.

Max was working behind the bar, serving an attractive young woman with short blonde hair. Katie's hackles immediately went up, despite the situation. Taking a deep breath, she moved into the lounge and found a secluded spot at the bar.

Max glanced over at her, but didn't stop his conversation with the blonde. He said something. The blonde laughed. And Katie felt like she'd just swallowed a battery.

Max mixed the woman a gin and tonic, set it before her, then moved across the bar to Katie.

"Hi," he said.

Just like that, all the jealousy was gone. It was Max in front of her, the man she loved.

"Hi."

"Can I get you anything?"

"Just tonic water, please. I had enough to drink last night to last me the rest of my life."

"Funny thing for the wife of a bar owner to say." He filled a glass with ice and tonic. "You look great."

"Thanks." She took a long sip of her drink, realizing just how thirty she was.

Before she could return the compliment, a man plopped himself into the stool beside her. He said, "Hey, couldn't help but notice you're alone."

Katie looked at Max, who'd faded back and resumed bartender mode. It was funny to Katie. To this guy, she was "alone." Max smiled too, just as amused by it. She drank the rest of her tonic before turning to her new suitor. He was a handsome Asian guy, about her age, tall, fit, and impeccably dressed. Not that he had a chance.

"You're an observant one." She shared a smile with her husband. "Did you also notice that my drink is empty?"

She lifted her glass with her left hand, making sure he saw her ring. The guy didn't seem fazed by either her marital status or her sarcasm. "I hadn't noticed. Want another?"

"I'm perfectly capable of paying for my own drinks." She waved Max over.

"Another?" Max said.

"Please. Oh, and Max, I'd like you to meet..." She looked at the guy.

"David," he said.

"David. David, this is my husband, Max."

The guy went white. "Sorry, man, I didn't realize..."

"What's that?" Max said.

David looked at Katie, then Max, then bolted for the door as fast as a man could and still maintain some dignity.

Katie and Max laughed.

"That was mean," Max said.

"He deserved it. He was making a mockery of our vows." It was her own joke, but it still came a little too close to home. "I'm sorry I didn't tell you about AJ as soon as it happened last week."

Max spread his hands out on the bar top and leaned forward, shoulders hunched. "Want to get out of here and talk about it?"

"Would love to. You have some place in mind?"

"Already have the boutique hotel booked," he said.

"You know, for a guy who claims he's not a planner, you seem to always have a plan."

Max shrugged. "All it takes is some motivation—and booking some private place where you can show me exactly what you did with AJ is pretty damn motivating."

Katie laughed. "Aren't you working?"

Max nodded. "But I've got someone to cover me. It's nice being the boss." He looked past her again. "And here he comes."

Katie turned, and there he was—AJ with a sheepish expression that looked out of place.

She whipped her head around to Max, eyes wide. Her husband grinned.

"I think you two may have met," Max said. "AJ, this is my wife, Katie. Katie, this is AJ."

"Hey, again," AJ said. For the first time since she'd met him, AJ looked cowed. Gone was the swagger. Gone was the cocky grin. He looked like a man who wanted to be anywhere but here.

Katie couldn't even manage a hello. She was too afraid it would come out as a squeak.

"Thanks for coming out here and taking over, AJ. You're a real trooper."

"No problem, boss."

Katie looked at Max in a way that she hadn't in a long time. She saw the command in him. She saw the power. These men were not equals, and despite the fact that AJ had fucked Katie last night, essentially behind Max's back, it was Max who controlled this situation. It made Max so sexy.

"Ready to get out of here?" Max asked her.

"Ready."

Max came around the bar, put his arm around Katie, and led her out of the bar. She could feel AJ's eyes on her as they left, but didn't dare look back.

****

Katie crossed over to the windows. Below her the Potomac River stretched out, the moon casting its pale reflection on the dark water. Katie laughed softly. "So by boutique, you meant one of the most upscale hotels in the city."

"It's all relative, right?"

"Technically, I don't think so," she said.

Max joined her at the window, placing a hand on her lower back. "For a second, I forgot who I was with. Okay then, technically, we can pretend not to be parents tonight."

Katie resisted the urge to explain to him that *pretending* made it decidedly not *technical*. Instead, she asked, "Are we married?"

"We don't have to be," Max said.

Katie turned and took Max in her arms. "I can't stop thinking about last night. You were such an animal...AJ."

Max inhaled sharply. He cupped her face, caressing her cheek. Katie liked it, but it served to remind her how different Max was from her lover last night. There was nothing tender about her younger lover.

"Tell me more," Max said. "What else did you like?"

Katie's breath came quick. "I loved the way you threw me on the bed and took me."

She bit her lip, looking up at Max. Was he going to do the same thing? Was he planning on acting it out?

He pulled her in for a hard kiss, pushing his tongue past her lips with passion. His other hand drew her against him, where she felt his hard-on press against her stomach.

"Were you naked?" he asked.

Katie nodded, happy that he'd decided to drop the role-play—for now, at least. He unzipped her dress and she pushed it off her shoulders, leaving her in a white lacy bra and matching thong.

Max checked her out, despite all the years between them, and she smiled inwardly at that. "AJ liked what he saw, too."

She unhooked the bra, remembering the way AJ had feasted on her tits. Max unbuttoned his black shirt, pulling it open. She touched the fine black curls on his pecs. Even though she knew she shouldn't, she compared him to AJ. AJ was fit in the way that a personal trainer should be fit, but as much as she liked his muscles, she'd go for Max's rugged masculinity every time.

Katie watched him the whole way to her knees. She went to work on his belt and zipper. "You liked it when I sucked your cock, too, didn't you?"

Max stared down at her, giving her a short nod. She freed his shaft and took it in her hand. Again, she compared. AJ was bigger, but Max was no slouch himself, and where AJ stretched the limits of comfort, Max was a perfect fit.

She ran the flat of her tongue along the underside, drawing a shudder. "You liked it when I did that," she said. "Or this." Taking him swiftly into her mouth, she sucked and swirled down the length until the spongy head hit the back of her throat. Then she sucked deeper.

Max groaned. "That feels so good." He placed a hand on her head, but didn't take control of her. Didn't face fuck her the way AJ had. Katie shivered at the memory.

AJ had been all over her as soon as the door was locked. He'd let Katie put her dress back on after their wild drive, but nothing else, so when he tore her dress off, all she had on beneath was her garter belt, stockings, and high heels. He'd stripped out of his clothes swiftly, thrown her onto the bed, face first, and taken her doggy style that first time. She'd been primed after blowing him as they raced down the highway. She needed cock, and needed it badly.

When he'd made her scream on the end of his glorious member, he'd pulled free, ripped the condom off, and forced her between his legs so that he could finish in her mouth. *Suck my cock, you horny slut,* he'd said. *I know how much you love to swallow my come.*

The worst thing was that she couldn't dispute him. She wasn't a huge fan of come—the taste wasn't great, and the consistency was too slimy to enjoy—but the idea of AJ using her like that, of forcing her to take him like he did, enflamed her like nothing else.

Her stomach fluttered at the naughty memory. She looked up at Max, back in the present, and wondered what he'd think about her if he could read her mind.

"Oh, baby, that feels so good."

Katie pulled off, a loud slurp ripping through the room. "You liked it even better when I did this," she said. Sitting up higher on her knees, she hefted her full breasts in the palms of her hands, wrapped them around Max's shaft, and squeezed.

Her husband groaned at the soft, warm sensation.

"You did that?" he said, his voice tight. He was close.

"Uh huh. You don't remember? You ordered me to. Told me that my tits were made for fucking."

Baby, show me what you can do with those tits. They're made to be fucked, was precisely what he'd said. He'd practically yanked her up by the hair to get her into position, but again, she'd loved it. She'd gotten so exciting watching AJ's curved manhood slide in and out of her cleavage. Every time she felt his shaved balls strike the underside of her breasts, it echoed in a throb between her legs. He'd looked down at her with such lust. Even now, it was thrilling to think about.

Max looked at her the same way, only she knew where his mind was. Like her, he was putting AJ in place of him. He was getting off on thinking of Katie slutting it up for another man.

"And when you were close, you made me beg for your come," she said. "You remember?"

"Oh, Katie..." Max's face was tight, his brow furrowed, his teeth clenched.

"Give me your come, AJ. Please, let me taste it. *Please...*"

Max's breath caught. Swiftly, Katie released his cock from her tits, wrapped her lips around it, and sucked down hard. He lasted half a second longer before exploding.

Katie swallowed, then kept sucking him until he pushed her away, too sensitive to take any more. He stumbled backward, sitting hard on the edge of the bed.

Katie sank to her knees, remembering where she was. Remembering that the man on the bed was her husband, not her lover—and that she still wanted Max to respect her in the morning.

Wiping her mouth, she rose, topless, her pale skin cast in moonlight.

"What happened next?" Max asked.

Katie couldn't tell where his head was at. Was he jealous? Was he hurt?

"Are you okay, Max?" She reached out to him, and was grateful when he took her hand.

"We're okay. More than okay. You're amazing, baby." He pulled her into his lap and kissed her.

"I don't feel amazing. I feel like a...like a slut."

"Well..." Max grinned. Katie laughed, shoving his arm. "Look," he said, "that's just it. You're amazing because you did that. And you didn't do it for me, or my fantasy—"

"Not entirely your fantasy, you mean."

"Right. You did this for you. I love that you let your passion consume you like that. Must be hard for an accountant to let go."

"Hey, now."

Max kissed her neck. "So what happened next? Tell me. I want to know everything."

Katie's stomach fluttered as she recalled AJ's next order. "He...he told me to play with myself. That he wanted to watch."

Max pulled back, his face bright. "Yes, please."

Katie felt more nervous at the idea of her husband watching her masturbate than she had last night. She'd been in the moment. She would have done almost anything AJ had told her to do.

She slipped out of Max's lap and crawled to the head of the bed, where a heap of pillows were piled. Reclining into them, she slipped her thumbs into her thong and dragged them down her thighs.

She spread her legs, watching him watch her. His breath came shallow. He barely blinked. He inhaled quickly as she pushed two fingers between her moist, pink lips.

"He asked me questions while I played for him," Katie said. Her thumb danced on her clit as she found her rhythm.

"Like what?"

"Like...have I ever cheated on you before."

"What did you tell him?"

"That I hadn't *cheated*. Ever."

"So you told him about our arrangement?" Max asked. His tone was cryptic, and Katie understood the delicacy of the situation now that she had more context. AJ worked for Max now, and that could get complicated if AJ knew about his boss's arrangement. Then again, no part of sleeping with the boss's wife was simple.

"I didn't," she said. "Not exactly. But I think that he understands. He's been with Nadia and John, after all."

"What else did he ask?" Max said.

"He asked me if I'd ever tasted myself. Then he told me to suck on my fingers."

"Do it," Max said.

Katie's heart skipped. She did as she was told, wrapping her lips around her two fingers like it was a cock.

"Do you like the way you taste?" Max asked.

Katie nodded.

He said, "Do you like the taste of pussy?"

Katie shuddered. AJ had asked the same, and she'd answered with a yes just to get a rise out of him.

"What else did he ask?"

"He asked if I'd ever been with two guys."

"You tell him you had?" Max asked.

"Uh huh."

"And?"

"He said he couldn't wait to share me. To fuck me while I sucked another guy's cock."

Max groaned.

"What did you say?"

Katie could have given a white lie, but she was done with the deception—even the little ones.

"I told him that I couldn't wait to do that with him." Her chest tightened as she realized she was going to tell him everything. "That I wanted to feel it from both ends."

Max crawled over her, cock in hand, at full strength. She pulled her fingers from her pussy, wrapped them around his shaft, and guided him into her. They groaned.

"I bet he liked your answer."

Katie moaned. "Yes, he...he did." She clawed at Max's back, urging him to take her harder. "He did the same thing you're doing now. He started fucking me again. Kept telling me how he couldn't wait to see that."

She was back in that moment again: her legs wrapped around AJ's muscular torso, his thick manhood splitting her, his balls striking her ass. And the things he said to her...

I can't fucking wait to see you take two guys at once...

She grabbed Max's back, drawing him close as she wrapped her legs around him.

I'm going to watch you swallow back-to-back cocks...

She arched back, pressing her tits against Max's chest as her memories assaulted her. His thrusts lifted her from the bed, just as

AJ's had.

Then, we're going to explode all over your face...

It was one of Katie's darkest fantasies, and AJ seemed to know every naughty detail of it

"Oh, Max, fuck me. Fuck...me!" Driving her heels into Max's back, she came hard, screaming out his name. Screaming for him to join her.

Max drilled her one last time, in and out, pinning her to the mattress. He covered her mouth with his, swallowing up her screams in a loose, passion-filled kiss.

"Uh!" He groaned, drawing back just enough to breathe. Their eyes met, her greens to his browns. She felt the connection, deep and profound.

And then he came and she tumbled into oblivion.

****

"So how did it all start?" Max asked.

They'd ordered room service since neither had actually had dinner—a salad for Katie, a cheeseburger for Max. Neither of them had bothered with clothes, although Max had donned a robe when answering the door.

Katie chose her words carefully, watching Max's reaction. "Well, it began at the holiday party..."

He furrowed his brow. Katie went on: "So you and AJ weren't the only ones I was with last night."

"No fucking way," he said.

Katie blushed, her embarrassment made real as she confessed just how naughty she'd been. Saying it out loud sounded so much worse than thinking it. "Bradley and I ended up in that little conference room I told you about."

"And?"

"And I gave him a satisfying farewell."

Max whistled. "You're full of surprises. Anything else you want to get off your chest?"

Katie laughed. "So you're not upset about any of it?"

"Are you?"

Katie thought about Bradley and the way she'd left him. In way, she was, but not for any of the reasons Max thought.

"Actually, I am." She sighed. "I think there's more Chloe in me than I've been honest about."

Max stiffened. "What?"

"Honest to myself, I mean. Not to you. For good or bad, Chloe Reynolds has a lot to do with the woman I've become. Not a great model, even if the model is one of sexual liberation. She's a manipulator. She uses people. And I've been doing all that."

"Katie, you're nothing like Chloe."

She felt tears well up in her eyes. She wiped them away. "But don't you see? I am. I could be. I didn't tell you about AJ. I worked across the street from him and I didn't tell you. Why? Because I selfishly wanted to keep that excitement for myself. I rationalized it away. I found reasons to justify the secrecy, but deep down, I knew it was wrong."

"And that's why you could never be Chloe," Max said. "You felt bad. Do you think she ever did?"

Katie's answer felt small. "No."

"And if you didn't, either, I'd say we have a problem. But here we are, having this conversation."

She squeezed Max close to her, tears streaming down her face. "You're too good for me, Max."

"Nah. I'm just as fucked up as you. You've got your *Chloe com-*

plex, or whatever. I've got this masochistic urge to send you off with other men."

She laughed through her sniffles, half-annoyed that he could cheer her up when all she wanted to do was feel sorry for herself. But that was the kind of guy he was, and she loved him so much for that.

"You know what's crazy? The last time we played this game, I got burned—*we* got burned. I know it was all a deception, but for me, for a short period there, I thought that I had lost you. I vowed that nothing was worth that risk."

"So did I," Katie said. The tears were turning into anger and self-loathing. "And that's why I can't *believe* I did what I did."

Max shook his head. "And yet we just spent the last hour fucking each other crazy as we re-enacted your night with my newest employee."

It was true. Absurd, but true. At first, Katie had nothing to say for that—no explanation. But then: "You know, there's something telling about that?"

"What's that?" Max asked.

She sniffed, starting to feel better. The tears were still there, but the crushing melancholy was mostly gone.

"The hottest part of last night's encounter wasn't last night, but right now. In the retelling. The reclaiming."

"Even for you?"

"Even for me." The moment she said it, she knew it was the profound, indisputable truth.

"Well then, I suppose you're just going to have to tell me about all your future encounters from now on."

"Yeah, I think I do." She said it like a tease, but they both felt the weight of the statement. "I love you, Max."

"I know. And God, do I love you."

They kissed. It felt fantastic. Cleansing. They were back again.

"So what are you going to do about AJ? About him working for you?"

"You mean am I going to fire him?" Max asked. "No, I won't do that. The more I've thought about it, this whole situation could actually be pretty fun."

She took a bite of salad, wondering what the hell that could mean. Then something occurred to her. "You asked him to text me, didn't you?"

Max colored, but he didn't look away. "I did."

"I was wondering how he had my number. So what was that? A test? I thought you trusted me."

He shook his head, but they both knew that it had been. "Just confirming something was all."

"How did he take that? When he found out who you were?"

Max chuckled. "Not as badly as I would have, probably. I get the feeling this isn't the first time he's had to deal with someone's husband."

"Probably not."

"We had a good, man-to-man talk. He knows where he stands now."

Katie thought about the sheepish look he had at the bar, and the way AJ had called Max *boss*. Max added, "Let's just say that he won't be calling me a cuck any time soon."

That made Katie laugh. The idea of Max in a cuckold role just didn't feel right, and yet Max clearly was into aspects of it. "You're a complicated man, Maxwell Callahan."

"Ditto, Katherine Callahan."

"So now that he has my number, think he'll be in touch?"

"After how you responded to him, I don't think so." He grinned.

"But I don't think we've seen the last of AJ."

Katie looked at him cock-eyed. "How do you mean?"

"You'll just have to wait and see."

CHAPTER 14

Christmas came and went in the whirlwind it always was. They opened presents. They had a Christmas roast. They wore silly sweaters, drank eggnog, and played Christmas music all day.

After that, Max focused on the upcoming New Year's Eve festivities, one of the busiest, and most lucrative, times of the year for bars. Katie took the week off to watch Mya.

AJ and Bradley faded like a dream—a hot, sexy dream that still made her feel tingly, but still just a dream. Only it wasn't, and she knew that sooner or later, she'd have to face the reality of it. Still, neither of them tried to contact her, and she was fine with that.

In January, she got a call from John Mitchell that immediately promised to make the New Year exciting—but in an entirely different way.

"So you remember how I said last year that I was working on a way to get back to DC?" he said.

"I do." Katie was at home when the call came in, dressed in her tight yoga digs. "Success?"

She missed her friend, and even though Nadia never said anything, Katie had the feeling that Nadia wasn't handling the long-distance marriage as well as she claimed.

"Almost."

"Anything I can do to help?" Katie asked. She always asked, and John always told her that there wasn't. This time, though...

"Actually, yes." He paused for dramatic effect. "Want to be a partner in a new firm?"

"New firm?"

"I was thinking Mitchell Callahan LLC." Katie could practically hear the smile in his voice. "Has a nice ring to it, doesn't it?"

Katie mouthed the name. *Mitchell Callahan.* She was only thirty. John was only a year older. Accountants their age didn't do this sort of thing. They hadn't put in their time.

Only they *had.* They'd been through the federal scandal. They'd weathered the worst audit in U.S. history, only to become experts in the field.

"Tell me more..."

John wasn't lying when he said that he was working hard to get something started while he was in New York. He didn't want to just come home and get another accountant gig at a large firm, though, or even a more senior position at a smaller one, like Katie had. He wanted to go big.

He'd called on his entire network, including his mentor in business school, and had put together a small team that could do what they'd excelled at—helping financial institutions navigate the convoluted regulations of the federal government. He'd pulled a few guys from the old team back in, lined up financial backers, and done almost all of the legwork. But there was one catch.

"This all hinges on you. They all agreed that they'd only go into this if you were on board."

It was a huge risk. Her current firm offered her stability and the potential for advancement down the road. John's offer had a much higher ceiling, but so much more uncertainty.

"Can I think about it?"

"Of course. Take your time. But Katie..."

"Yeah?"

"It's not just the backers that need you. Or the team. Or the clients." He sighed. "I need you, too."

Katie's heart skipped. Hearing John say that meant a lot. She'd mentored him while they'd worked together, but in the last year, his potential had turned into reality. She'd begun to hear his name thrown around as a rising star.

She also quite liked the idea that he *needed* her. She still remembered Halloween. If they worked with one another again, she wouldn't mind doing that again, either.

"Okay, let me talk it over with Max. I'll get back to you quickly."

"Sounds good."

"Thanks for thinking of me, John."

"Always."

****

"I *bet* he wants to work with you," Max said with a laugh.

Katie rolled her eyes. Of course his mind would go there. "It's not like that."

"But it kind of is, isn't it?"

She'd gone to yoga after all, just to let her mind work through the intricacies of this new development. By the time she'd emerged, relaxed in both body and mind, she knew what she wanted to do.

"Can we focus on the business side of this thing?" Katie said.

"Sure. I think you should go for it," he said.

"Just like that? Don't you want to hear more of the details?"

"Does it require you moving to New York?" Max asked.

"I'd have to travel up there occasionally for client meetings, but no. We'd be located here."

"Then I don't have a problem with it."

"How can you be so blasé about this?" Katie said. Sometimes, Max's casual attitude towards life annoyed her. She wondered how on earth he could be so successful as a bar owner.

Max took her by the shoulders and looked her right in the eyes. "You want to do this. I can tell. And I think you'd always regret it if you didn't. I'd rather you try and fail than not."

"Says the guy who's never failed."

Max grinned. "What can I say? I'm the luckiest guy I know. Now, want to go upstairs and celebrate this opportunity?"

He slipped his hands down her back and over her tight, Lycra pants.

"That *would* help clear my head a little more," she said.

****

Things moved quickly after that. John lined up the backers and scheduled a meet and greet in New York on February 1.

"You sure you can't come?" Katie asked Max as he carried her suitcase down the stairs.

"I'll be there in spirit," he said, kissing her at the door. When she pulled back and looked at him, she swore she caught a hint of mischief in his face.

"You're up to something."

Max laughed. "Please. Me? Never."

"Uh huh."

"Good luck, honey. Remember, they all asked for *you*. Just be yourself."

And with that, she was on her way up to New York.

John met her at Grand Central Station, looking dressed down yet professional—slacks, neatly tucked dress shirt, no tie. Still, her mind jumped to another version of John—one that involved him naked, his cock still wet from her pussy.

She shook her head to clear it, but saw that John had to do the same. Their eyes met and they shared a laugh. "It's good to see you, Katie."

Katie pulled him into a hug. "You too, John. So where are you taking me to dinner?"

"Oh, I'm taking you to dinner?" he said with a laugh. "Doesn't the mentor usually pick up the tab?"

"We're about to be partners, John. We're equals."

"Then let's find some place and split the check." He smiled. "Partner."

Katie liked John. He was Good People. They could talk about the technicalities in the accounting world, but in an evolution of their friendship, they could touch on the more intimate side of Katie's world—the one that only a few knew about.

"So how are things with you and Max?" he asked. They'd found a hole-in-the-wall Thai place on the Upper West Side. It was exactly what she was in the mood for—some place where she could relax, not worry about changing out of her jeans, and still enjoy great food.

"We're good. Thanks for watching Mya back in December. That was…that was awesome."

"Nothing you wouldn't do for me or Nadia."

"Of course."

"So everything's cleared up now?"

"Yeah. I was being stupid, but we're straight now." Katie gave him an abbreviated version of December events, from the fast and furious tour-turned-sex at City Fitness to the IMBARK holiday party to sex down 66. Laying it all out like that, every mistake she'd made became amplified. As always, though, John listened to it all without judgment.

"You are one sexy lady, Katie. Max is lucky to have you."

"More like I'm lucky to have him." She sighed. "I don't know why I didn't tell him the first time it happened."

"Sounds like you did," John said. "You just didn't say who it was you were with."

"A lie of omission is still a lie."

"If it's a malicious one. But I don't think you meant to harm Max with this one. It just excited you some, to have this secret little affair with AJ."

"But that's wrong," Katie said. "I shouldn't have *anything* that constitutes an *affair*. That's when people start getting hurt."

"Okay, maybe *affair* isn't the right word, so let's not argue semantics. What I'm saying is that the intent isn't to do something behind his back because he would object to it. You said it yourself—nothing's off-limits with him, as long as you're using your best judgment. He trusts you. But sometimes, full disclosure can suck all the excitement out of a thing."

"And sometimes, it's just not worth the risk. Just because he said that nothing was off-limits doesn't mean he actually meant it. Not deep down. We don't always know ourselves." She thought about what Max had deemed her *Chloe complex* and laughed to herself.

"Besides, you and Nadia don't have any secrets."

John's eyes glanced into her cleavage, quickly but not quickly enough that she didn't catch him. "Well, I haven't told Nadia that I'm madly in love with you."

For a second, Katie froze. Then, she saw his smile and relaxed.

"So we started playing this game with each other when I moved up here and she stayed behind. Basically, Nadia hooks up with someone and doesn't tell me about it. The catch is that she leaves all these clues that she's doing it."

"Really?" Katie was shocked. That sounded so wrong. "Like what kind of clues?"

"Oh, I don't know. Like, when she was up in New York, visiting, she'd leave her phone out long enough to let me see a suggestive text from a guy. Or she'd make sure that when she dressed, I caught a glimpse of her new bra or something."

Katie tried putting herself in John's shoes. She thought of Max hinting at something going on behind her back. Like, he'd tell her that he was closing up the restaurant, only to come home smelling like perfume. It made her cringe.

"I don't know that we could do that," she said, then added: "Why would anyone do that? Seems so reckless."

John held up his hands, palms out. "Isn't there some saying about sinners throwing stones?"

"*Let he without sin cast the first stone*, I believe," Katie said. She laughed. "Good thing I'm not a *he*."

"Totally a good thing."

Katie rolled her eyes, but couldn't stop smiling. "Don't you get jealous?"

"Oh yeah. Really jealous. But that's the whole point. It's a game that plays with that emotion." He paused in thought. "We've got some strange kinks, don't we, and emotions can be powerful things. Nadia's tapped into mine like no one I've ever known before. In a way, it sounds like you've tapped into Max's."

"I don't know that we could play your game. We have history."

John nodded. "And based on what you've told me, I don't think that it's a game that would be good for you guys. But also remember that history is history. Don't let it be a burden on everything. You'll have so much more fun that way."

****

The big meeting with their investors went well, although Katie felt rusty doing all the schmoozing. It wasn't required at the small firm she'd been working for. They already had an established base of clients, and the ones that they did have were like IMBARK—small and non-profit. A glass of wine and an hour in, though, and she was back in full form.

Not that she needed it. They were ready to go the moment she set foot in the rented meeting space in her Prada business suit. John had primed them well. They just needed her to tell them where to sign.

"I've heard a lot about you, Katie," said one of the investors.

"Thanks a lot, Roger," Katie said with the same confidence. "I've heard good things about you, too. How's commercial real estate doing in DC?"

Roger seemed pleased that she really did know who he was. Of course she did. Katie had spent the better part of a month studying up on her investors and potential clients. Roger Hensley was CEO of Lattice LLC, a major player in commercial real estate throughout the southeastern U.S. and one of their major backers.

"It's been better, but things are slowly turning around. It's like this, though. Everything's a cycle."

Katie couldn't help thinking about Max as he said it—about their marriage and the ups and downs. The last couple years had certainly presented that.

"Tell me about it," Katie said. "If you'd told me a few years ago that I would be starting my own firm, I would have assumed you were drunk."

Roger chuckled. "Not nearly drunk enough," he said, raising his empty glass of wine.

"Let's go fix that."

The rest of the afternoon was spent getting to know one another, talking to new clients, and setting up meetings in the future. John took her out to dinner with one of their biggest clients, a guy named Adrian Krause.

Adrian represented a defense contractor who'd be a major coup for an upstart firm to grab. He was also a pretty good-looking guy, and while Katie prided herself on using her abilities and her experience as major selling points, she didn't mind all the eye contact and the way he touched her arm when making his points.

She also didn't miss the fact that John noticed the subtle flirtation as well. The first time she looked over at John as Adrian put a hand on her elbow and caught her new partner's eyes dart away, she didn't think much of it. Then she noticed it again. And again.

When Adrian left, John turned to her and said, "He was… friendly," everything clicked.

"You're jealous," Katie said, covering her mouth as she laughed.

"Don't be silly," he said, color springing to his cheeks.

"You totally are."

"Why would I be jealous?"

"You tell me," Katie said. She hooked her arms in his and guided him down the street. "Come on, let's walk back to the hotel. It's only a few short blocks."

They walked arm-in-arm in silence, oblivious to the chilly February night. They'd done it. Mitchell Callahan LLC was no longer just an idea. Katie felt the same sense of recklessness that she had when she'd gone out on a date with Greg, way back when. It made her horny.

"I think it's cute, you know," Katie said at last. "That I made you jealous."

"I wasn't—"

"So if I told you that while you were in the bathroom, he invited me up to his room, that wouldn't make you feel anything in particular?" She felt John stiffen—confirmation enough.

"It would make me question your professionalism, maybe."

Katie thought about Bradley and the line she'd crossed there. This time, it was Katie who felt the embarrassment.

John realized the implication. "I'm sorry, I didn't mean that."

"No, you're right." Katie stopped, turned to him, and took his hands in hers. "That was a mistake I won't make again. I promise."

"Okay." He looked so handsome—her partner, her lover. She smiled, adding, "But it still made you jealous."

"Fine, maybe a little." He didn't slow down. He didn't slip his hand into hers. But she felt the intimacy between them grow. When he spoke, his voice was slow and measured. "You know what we really should do to celebrate?"

The air around them crackled with electricity.

Katie could have easily taken him up on his offer. History made him safe.

But history also made no one safe.

"I'm sorry. I can't. Not tonight."

John nodded. "I understand."

"Things are still complicated."

"Believe me, I understand, and it's okay." He pulled her close and kissed her on the cheek. "Congrats, partner. The future's all possibility."

Katie smiled up at him. "I love it."

****

"Hey, Max," Katie said. She called him as soon as she entered her hotel room.

"You did it!" Max shouted down the line.

Katie laughed at his enthusiasm. It was all a big rubber stamp, but she couldn't help feeling the same way. "We did."

"Party time."

"Yeah, that's what I was thinking, too. Wish you were here."

He said, "Me, too."

Now that she was actually talking to Max, things didn't seem as easy as they had when she'd worked through them on the walk back to the hotel. They felt more delicate than just coming out and saying, *So...I was wondering if you'd be cool if I fucked John.* There was history to consider.

"The last time we were apart, I was on the other side of the world," Katie said carefully.

"And I was tearing myself up with jealousy and despair."

"You feel like that now?"

"Not even close," Max said. "That doesn't mean my imagination's not working through some...possibilities."

And just like that, Max was able to diffuse all the tension she felt. "So if I told you that John was on his way up to my room?"

"I'd ask for pictures to prove it."

Katie's heart quickened.

Max said, "What are you wearing, Katie?"

"The Prada suit," she said. She wandered in front of the full-length mirror, giving herself the same once-over that Roger Hensley and Adrian Krause had earlier. She saw what they saw—a sexy, confident corporate exec. Her burnished auburn locks were held off her face in a high ponytail. Her make-up still looked good, lips glossy, mascara dark, eye shadow sparkling.

"I love that suit," Max said. "But why don't you take it off? For John, I mean."

Katie watched herself laugh in the mirror. She realized that Max didn't really believe her. Still, her hand drifted to the buttons of her jacket. She shifted her phone from ear to ear as she shucked it off.

He must have heard the muffling of clothes being removed. "I bet you're wearing something dirty underneath, aren't you?"

Her skirt went next, exposing her thigh highs. "I am."

"Something new?"

She undid the buttons down her black blouse. Beneath, she wore a black bra and matching thong. She traced the edge of the bra, which was lined with delicate, white lace. "No, not new. It's the 'French maid' set you like so much."

"Very sexy. Garter belt?"

Katie touched the tops of her hosiery. "Not tonight. Thigh-highs though. The nude ones."

"And your shoes?"

Katie turned her back to the mirror and checked herself out. Her tall pumps made her butt look great. "The black Christian Louboutins. With the red soles."

"Classy, yet kind of slutty. I like it."

"Hold on," she said. Pulling the phone away, she started up the camera app and took a photo of herself in the mirror, blowing a kiss over her shoulder. She quickly loaded it into a text message and sent it off to her husband.

"A present for my dear husband," she said, phone back up to her ear.

A moment later, Max said, "Wow. Now I really wish that I was there."

"Me too." Katie ran her fingers down between her legs, pushing them beneath her thong. She'd started to warm up, her pussy moist enough to coat her fingers. "Good thing I've got John."

"Good thing," Max said.

Did he still not believe her? She felt a stubborn impulse to set the record straight. She already knew that this wouldn't be the last photo she'd be taking that night.

A knock at the door startled her out of her thoughts. A quick glance at her state of undress had her adrenaline up. "Hold on. There's someone at my door?" Her upward inflection turned the statement into a question.

"You should check on that."

Something about Max's suggestion had her suspicions on the rise. She pulled on a hotel robe, tied it closely her body, and went to the peephole. The man on the other side got her heart racing in a hurry. She pulled back, whispering into the phone: "Max, you're behind this, aren't you?"

"What's that now? Who's at the door?" She could hear the smile in his voice.

"You know perfectly well who it is."

"It's a big day," Max said. "You don't like my present?"

"You know, you could have sent me flowers."

Max laughed. "Now that would have been boring."

"Wouldn't want that."

"Have fun tonight, Katie. And if you want to take a few more pictures, I won't complain."

"Well that's a relief." She laughed. "Good night, Max."

"Good night, baby. I love you."

"I love you, too. And thanks for the...flowers."

"Ha." Click.

Another knock came at the door. Katie jumped at it, forcing her breathing under control. Eyes closed, she steadied her hand and opened the door. "Well this is a surprise, AJ," she said with a smile. "Long way from home."

CHAPTER 15

AJ gave her a toothy grin. "I'm here to deliver your purse. You left it down in the bar."

His hands were empty. His smile grew.

Her head spun a little with the déjà vu of this exchange. Was it Max's idea for her to play out the hypothetical of her first encounter with AJ? Or was that something the trainer came up with on his own? It didn't matter.

"How careless of me. Thanks for bringing it up." She stepped aside, letting him in. "Such a gentleman."

AJ stepped inside the doorframe, but stopped when he was right next to her. He glanced down at her. She could feel the heat rise off his body through his shirt. She could smell the cologne he wore, and the musk of sweat and masculinity beneath that.

"How about a reward for my good deed?"

"What did you have in mind?"

They shared a smile. Then he leaned in and kissed her.

The kiss was hungry. Possessive. His hand curled behind her

neck, pulling her mouth up to his as he smothered her lips. She clutched his shirt, feeling his solid body beneath her knuckles. When he drew back, she was out of breath, punch drunk and woozy.

"That'll do to start," he said. Finally, they shut the door. Practically before it had finished clicking shut, they were in each other's arms again, mouths crashing together again. She'd fucked this man. She'd sucked his cock in a moving vehicle. And yet despite all that, kissing him felt profoundly intimate.

"What have you got under here?" AJ asked. He reached for the belt of her robe. She let him pull it open, enjoying the ravenous way he processed the lacy underthings. "Fuck, you're a hottie."

A hottie. Under normal circumstances, it's not something she liked being called. But with AJ, the paradigms were all different.

When he was done drinking in her bare skin and the way her bra and panties clung to her, he reached out and set a broad hand on her neck again. But this time, rather than pull her close for a kiss, he put enough downward pressure on her for her to take a hint. "For part two of my reward..." he said.

Katie sank to her knees, looking up at him through her long lashes. She loved the challenge of this position—how to turn a gesture of servitude into one of power. AJ stroked her cheek from above, his dark eyes never wavering from her. He gave a short nod, and she went to work on his belt. She let him think he was in control.

This guy was not her superior. She was older than him, more successful than him, more ambitious. Not to mention that he worked for her husband—was even in this hotel room because her husband had told him to be there.

"That's it, baby. I've missed that pretty little mouth of yours."

Katie took a shuddering breath. *Okay, so playing the submissive could be plenty sexy.*

Dipping in, she took the bulbous head between her lips, sucking firmly as she swirled his glans with her tongue. He groaned. Adjusting his stance, placing his feet slightly wider, he seemed to prepare for her best. She obliged that.

"Oh, babe. Look at you go." Katie danced along his length, filling the room with the frothy sounds of a good blowjob. She used both hands on what she couldn't reach, twisting and stroking in time with her bobs.

"I can't wait to fuck you until you scream," he said. "You ready to scream?"

Katie moaned around his shaft. She loved the idea. She tried pulling off, to move things to the bed, but he held her in place.

"Not so fast, slut. First things first, I'm going to watch you swallow my come. Then we can get on to your screaming."

With that incentive, she redoubled her effort on his shaft. She blew him until her jaw began to ache and her throat felt raw. She pulled off him, dribbling kisses down his length, and lapped at his balls—all the while stroking him.

"You like that?" she asked. "You like having your balls sucked?"

AJ groaned at the question. It was answer enough. She took the shaved sack into her mouth, tonguing his balls as she sucked on them. His hand flew into her hair, forming a fist that sent a flash of pain across her scalp.

"Oh, fuck," he moaned.

Katie didn't let up on the onslaught—physical or verbal. She reached behind her, unsnapping her bra. "Or would you prefer my tits?"

"Uhn, Katie…"

Collecting her hefty breasts, she wrapped them around his saliva-bathed length. The sight of his girthy cockhead jutting out of her cleavage took her breath away. It nearly did AJ in.

"You like that?" she asked. She tit-fucked him, undulating her entire body to maximize the fleshy strokes. "I like it, too. Makes me so horny, feeling your big, hard cock between my tits."

Her dirty words had their intended effect. She watched his eyes go flat and his breath catch. She smothered his cock one last time before shifting it back into her mouth. He exploded a moment later, filling her mouth with his hot seed.

She swallowed it all, feeling her body warm and abuzz with her own imminent climax. She basked in the euphoria without pushing for more. More would come later. So much more.

Looking up at him coyly, she said, "Your turn."

She stood, taking AJ by the hand and guiding him to the bed. She threw herself onto it, climbing into the mound of pillows. AJ watched her shimmy out of her thong, leaving her naked but for her stockings. Only then did he pull his shirt off and join her on the bed. On his stomach, his muscular body stretched out, he reminded her of a lion, powerful, yet content to lounge. He lowered his head to her pussy.

His tongue touched her exposed clit, scrambling her brain. She closed her eyes and arched her back. AJ had smooth cheeks and no stubble, and she was grateful for that. He also had a broad tongue, fitting for a man of his stature, and it felt fucking amazing as it passed across her sensitive lips.

Vaguely, she thought she caught the double beep of the hotel's electronic lock. AJ's mouth kept her from processing it until she heard someone say, "Well, looks like they started without us."

Katie's chest tightened. She shot a glance at the door, just in time to see it swing shut. There, as though stepping from a dream, was Max. For a second, she thought that it *was* a dream. Or at the very least, a hallucination.

Then she saw John behind him.

"Max?"

"This a bad time? Don't let me interrupt."

AJ didn't stop eating her, which Katie would have realized was significant if the higher functioning portions of her brain weren't so fuzzy. Instead, the man pushed two fingers inside her and the world listed.

She blinked, and Max was right there beside her. His weight made the bed shift, which made him real.

"You're here," she said.

He touched her face, brushing a sweaty lock of auburn hair off her forehead. "Of course I'm here. This is one of the most important days of your life."

"But I thought—"

"Want to make it one of the most memorable nights, too?"

Before she could answer, he kissed her, long and deep. She reached up, touching his face gingerly at first. If he *were* a hallucination, she wanted it to last as long as possible. When he didn't vanish right away, though, she threaded her fingers through his curly hair and pulled him deeper into the kiss.

Max pulled back, smiling. "Now, didn't you say something about a threesome fantasy with AJ?"

AJ ate her faster, spurred on by the mention of his name. Max faded back further, lifting his phone. "Enjoy, Katie."

On her other side, she felt John's weight on the bed. It took her breath away. She looked at Max one last time, questioningly. He just smiled and nodded.

Katie turned and found her new partner there, naked and a touch shy. "Hey, you knew all along?"

John shrugged, but nodded. "Sorry, didn't want to give away the surprise."

His kiss was familiar in the way that an old vice was—like the first drag of a cigarette after a long absence, or the way she imagined an encounter with Chloe and Greg would be if she could look past her anger.

He kissed along her jaw and into the tender space behind her ear, his hand collecting her left breast. She moaned as he thumbed her nipple. Things started to get overwhelming.

"Enjoy yourself, Kates," John whispered into her ear. A moment later, he kissed down her chest, collected both tits in his hands, and tongued her nipples.

She lost it. The sensation of two mouths on her, of four hands, of the thought of two hard cocks, and her brain couldn't keep up. She arched against John, barking out a moan. She wrapped her thighs around AJ's head and squeezed. He didn't let up. He continued to eat her, lashing away at her swollen pussy as she rocketed through her orgasm.

The men didn't let her come down. Not fully. Before she could get her feet back on the ground, they switched. John went to work on her pussy, his mouth less demanding and more familiar than AJ's. AJ mauled her tits, bringing the attack to her sensitive nipples. The shift pushed her close to another orgasm.

She looked over at her husband, who was sitting in the hotel room's desk chair. He was naked, although he wasn't touching himself. He just stared with an expression somewhere between excited and totally fucking overwhelmed. When he saw her looking, he nodded. "That good?"

"Yes," she hissed.

Katie was barely able to breathe, let alone comprehend what

came next. John pushed two fingers into her pussy, sending another toe-curling wave of pleasure through her. His tongue flickered across her pussy as AJ dipped low and did the same to her swollen nipples. She laced her fingers through his hair and moaned.

The sense of being the center of attention was exhilarating. They were here to please her, to use her, to possess her until she had nothing left to give. She never realized how sexy that idea was until that moment, as two men got her off with their hands and mouths.

Then AJ and John escalated things. As if they had some mental connection, AJ pulled off her at the same time as John. Katie moaned in protest, but their absence was short lived. John flipped her onto her stomach, lifting her ass.

"Onto your hands and knees," AJ said. "Time to show us how well you take two guys at once."

Katie's pulse jumped. Her body shook. This was so wrong. Just a few hours earlier, she was entertaining high profile corporate execs who believed in her professional acumen. Now, she was about to be filled from both ends by a couple guys who were not her husband—as her husband looked on! It set fire to her world.

"Oh my God!" she cried as John entered her from behind. "Ngh—"

Katie buried her face in the pillow, her moans more growls than cries. She raised her ass higher, changing the angle of the cock pounding her from behind. So good. So full...

She turned her head enough to breathe, her red hair spilling across her face, sticky with sweat. She caught sight of Max again. He was on his feet now, cock in one hand, the phone in the other. He was filming this! The realization sizzled through her.

"Harder." Her voice cracked. "Harder!"

"You're so sexy," John groaned, his voice faltering under the strain.

"He's not lying," AJ said above her. She looked up, only to find his thick cock in her face.

She swallowed every inch of the cock being fed to her.

"That's it, babe. Suck my cock while you get fucked from behind."

John began pumping faster, matching the fevered rhythm of her messy blowjob.

"Yeah, like that. Fuck this slut. Give it to her."

Katie's ears burned. Her face burned. Her whole body fucking burned. She swirled her head and thrust her hips back, taking the cocks at once. Helping them sync. And when they did—when their thrusts lined up and they entered her at the same time, she nearly lost it. To be filled like that, to be at the center of so much hard, sexy masculinity, she was a brightly burning filament of a light bulb, ready to pop.

Katie mutedly heard John's voice behind her: "She's going to go again."

"You?" AJ asked.

"I'm close."

"Switch?" AJ asked.

Before Katie's hazy brain could catch up, they were pulling out of her, flipping her onto her back. John fed his cock into her mouth from above. AJ slotted his curved manhood into her well-fucked pussy. Somewhere in her sex-addled brain, something registered as wrong, but she couldn't grasp it. A moment later, AJ's grunt put a name to it.

"Fuck, you feel so good. I love a bare, tight cunt."

Bare. Bareback. He wasn't wearing a condom. He couldn't have had time. And the cock in her mouth—John's cock—didn't taste like spermicide or latex or anything but warm, slippery cock.

She thought of Max to her left, watching. He'd known and hadn't stopped it. He would have if he'd had a problem with it, right? The sensation of the two men made it hard to think it through and impossible to stop. But maybe she didn't *want* them to stop. Not deep down. She wanted to feel AJ explode inside her. She wanted to be that nasty.

That tipped her over the edge. She lost the thread of what was happening to her. With the cocks inside her. With the pleasure she was feeling. With her mouth full of John's cock, she screamed.

"Uh, Kates," John said, he voice tight. "I'm close…"

Her moans raced down his length. He groaned, sinking down into her, driving his cock against the back of her throat. She gagged. Fear seized her. Fear that she'd choke. That she'd drown herself on another man's come.

John pulled back at the last second, exploding inside her mouth. She swallowed, but come escaped the corners of her mouth, its warmth dribbling down her neck. It was raunchy and gross and so thrillingly hot that she nearly came all over again.

AJ kept the orgasms rolling. John pulled back, and there was AJ, fucking her missionary. Now that he had her solo, he really gave it to her.

"Take it, baby. Feel my cock. Love it."

She looked down, where his smooth shaven cock met her waxed pussy. No condom. The thrill of it struck her like a blow to the stomach. Sensing her anxiety, he said, "I'm clean. I have papers. Your husband insisted on it from us both."

Katie snapped her head to Max, who nodded confirmation.

She mouthed a *thank you* before AJ escalated things into the final lap. He lifted her legs over his broad shoulders, folding her in half as he pounded into her. She stopped thinking about Max. Or the camera. Or anything at all but for the thrilling feel of AJ's bareback girth filling her, moving closer and closer to an unprotected end.

"You feel so...uh!" She couldn't focus enough to even talk dirty. She tried again. "Feel so fucking good, AJ. Fuck. Me!"

Each long stroke teased her g-spot with the crown of his cock-head. She'd never felt anything like it. This man was not only skilled at fucking, but he seemed designed by nature to do just that. She clawed at the bed sheets as she crashed through orgasm after orgasm. She didn't even realize she'd been screaming until she couldn't anymore, her throat raw.

"Uh, babe, look at you. So fucking hot," AJ said, pulling back enough to survey her sweat-covered body.

Katie tried to return the compliment. With that hard, muscled body, deeply tanned and toned to absolute perfection, he was eye-candy, a guilty pleasure that she never would have indulged in when she was younger, but couldn't wait to repeat now that she had.

He pulled free from her, his hand taking over the stroking as he pointed it across her stomach and chest. Her breath caught. She gasped, preparing for the messy finish.

He exploded across her tits and stomach, firing in syrupy bursts. A rope of come striking her neck. Another landed in her cleavage. Yet another dribbled into her navel, trickling toward her smooth shaven cunt.

AJ gave a great grunt as he settled back onto his haunches, finally spent. Katie closed her eyes and looked up at the ceiling, completely satiated.

****

Max and Katie dragged themselves into the shower. AJ and

John hung back, giving her some space with her husband. That subtle acquiescence wasn't lost on Katie. Strangely, for a dominant personality like AJ, he knew his role in her life.

Once the come had been washed away, Max held her under the shower spray, kissing her. "So you really didn't think I'd come?"

"No," Katie laughed.

"You've never missed one of my bar openings—not even the last one. What makes you think I'd miss this?"

"I hadn't thought of it like that." Katie touched his face. "You're so sweet."

"So orchestrating a threesome with two other guys is now considered sweet?"

"We've come a long way, haven't we, Max?" Katie giggled. "You know what the best part of tonight was? You watching."

"That was my favorite part, too," Max said with a smile. "But Katie, I was wondering...want to see what happens when I do more than just watch?"

"What did you have in mind?"

Max drew her into his arms, his hands moving around to her ass. "Something *really* naughty."

Katie didn't know what he was referring to. She started to ask him when she felt a finger press against her asshole. Her knees buckled. Her moan escaped before she could hold it in.

"We've never done that..." She drew a ragged breath.

"No time like the present...when it involves three horny guys."

The idea was so wrong, yet instantly irresistible. Max's finger penetrated her ass. It felt gigantic. How was she ever going to fit a cock in there?

"Just relax, Katie. Let it go. Whatever you're thinking, stop that and breathe..."

Max's lips touched down on her neck. His free hand slide down between her legs and pushed into her pussy. She rocked forward, resting her head against Max's shoulder as she came with a scream.

She clutched Max to her. He was her rock to crash against. He was her constant. He'd always be her constant. No matter how crazy life would get, she could count on him being there for her.

Her emotions came on, raw and unadulterated. She'd almost lost this man. Again. Never again. Never. Again.

Drawing back, she stared up at him, shifting from pupil to pupil. He looked blurry through her tears, but still the man she'd said *I do* to. The man she'd pledged to spend the rest of her life with.

"Thank you for coming up here," Katie said. She hadn't known what was missing until he'd arrived, she thought at first, then said it aloud. "You being here makes this moment just perfect."

"Sounds pretty sentimental for an accountant."

"Pretty sure that's all your fault."

"Fair. I'll take that," he said. "So ready to do something really crazy?"

"As long as you're there to watch."

Max laughed. "Oh, I'm done watching."

"Well then, Max, tonight…" She put her hands on Max's shoulders and looked him in the eyes. "Tonight, nothing's forbidden."

They shared a laugh, a kiss, exited the shower as one.

CODA

They shut off the shower, toweling each other off in between kisses. She still hadn't had a chance to fully comprehend where this was going, because the moment she did, she wasn't sure she could follow through.

In the bedroom, Max gave the other two guys a subtle nod. John sprang into action, pulling her to the bed and positioning her against the pillows. He looked up at her, his smile wide and familiar, and tongued her slit.

Katie groaned, eyelids drooping at the warm and wet sensation. She cupped her breasts and ran circles around her nipples.

She shut her eyes, releasing one of her tits so she could run her fingers through John's hair. He swirled her clit in a chaotic, tangled pattern that left her on edge. The room felt like it didn't have enough air for the four of them. She sucked it down, but couldn't seem to get enough.

"Ah, here we are," she heard Max say without it registering.

John flicked his tongue faster, pumped his fingers harder. His knuckles grazed the base of her clit, drawing a sharp moan from her.

She heard a buzzing off to her left. Her ears burned at the sound. Max said, "Here, use this."

Katie's world lagged. She composed a reply in her head—*Thanks, but I'm good*—but by the time it made it to her mouth, she realized that the offer wasn't for her. John's fingers left her for a fleeting, empty moment. Then she felt the cool sensation of lube being drizzled along her ass. A moment later, the press of her vibrating dildo filled the void left by John's fingers.

Katie arched. She threw her legs over John's back and arched up as he pushed the vibrator into her cunt. It felt huge. It felt so wrong. And it felt fucking incredible.

Katie's loud shout was something between a cry and a moan. Her world was reduced to the single point of contact where the vibrator entered her. Nothing else mattered. It buzzed. It dipped in and out, stretching her, prepping her. And when her orgasm came on, fast and wet, it obliterating everything.

"She's nice and primed." John's voice floated around her, slippery and detached.

"I heard," Max said. "You ready to do this?"

In the haze, Katie felt herself being adjusted. Positioned. Someone flipped her over—capable hands that lingered wherever they touched. She felt lips on her collarbone. On her neck. On her nipples. She was lifted over legs. AJ's or John's, she didn't know. She didn't care.

Straddling one man, she felt the hard press of a cock against her pussy. Hands lowered her hips. She sank down on to it, feeling it spread her. Fill her so good. AJ. That monstrous cock inside her was AJ's. If the girth hadn't been a giveaway, the pressure it put on her g-spot would have been.

AJ groaned. "That's so good."

She couldn't seem to open her eyes. Didn't want to. Her body was buzzing. Buzzing. Buzzing.

The vibrator was buzzing again. She felt a hand on her back, pressing her into a deep straddle over AJ. She went with it, her rich, wet hair falling across AJ's chest. Caressing his jaw and chin, she reveled in the moment. And then—

"Gah!" Katie stiffened as she felt the vibrator against her anus.

She came. Or maybe she'd never fully stopped coming since John ate her pussy. All she knew was that the sensations touching down on her asshole were more intense than anything she'd felt in her life—and things were about to get a whole lot crazier.

"I knew you'd like that," AJ said.

Her body purred, although whether that was from her orgasm or the vibrator, she didn't know. She certainly didn't care.

"Your wife's got a dirty side to her," AJ said.

"Tell me about it." Max put more pressure on the vibrator. She felt it spread her cheeks, tantalizingly close to entering her. Pain seared through her, but there were equal parts pleasure there.

"Just relax," Max whispered.

Katie drew on her yoga classes. She'd always loved the measured *pranayama* breathing exercises some of the teachers taught. She tried recalling all of them now. She focused on diaphragmatic inhalations, calming herself, getting her body back in control.

That wasn't so easy with the frenetic prodding against her asshole.

When Max pulled back, though, for a brief, confusing moment, she wondered if she'd willed the sensations away with her breathing. Then she felt something cool and slippery drip across her backside. The lube again.

She tensed before she could remember not to. Every part of her clenched—her muscles, her mind, her sense of self. She'd never had anal sex before. Never even really thought it was something she wanted to do. Only now, hundreds of miles away from home, in a room with three guys ready to fuck her, she couldn't wait to get ass fucked.

Max pressed his cockhead against her sphincter and simple things like speaking and thinking became impossible. If she hadn't been rolling through orgasms before, now they came. And came and came.

At some point, the pain was back, a ring of fire that turned her moans into ragged cries. She forgot her breathing techniques. She forgot to breathe at all. All she could think about the filling sensation of Max's cock entering her ass.

And AJ's huge cock curving thickly across her g-spot.

And—*oh yes*—John right beside them, filming the lewd act.

She didn't even realize that she'd been yelling, "Oh my God!" over and over until her throat was so raw that she couldn't any more. But *Oh my God* did she feel full. And only then did AJ start to move inside her again.

Max sank into Katie's virgin ass tenderly, taking his time—his agonizingly slow time. At some point between the moment he entered her and the moment he was all the way in, the pain fell away—mostly—replaced by euphoria. It was that nicotine buzz times a thousand.

When he was buried ball deep inside her, he said, "You ready?"

Katie laughed at the absurd question. "Do I have a choice?"

"You've always got a choice."

Nothing was forbidden, indeed.

Katie lost track of time. Minutes. Hours. Days. It all lost meaning before the intense and profound sense of being *filled*. They found a rhythm, one entering her as the other withdrew. In and out, never giving her a moment to rest. She always had a cock deep—really deep.

But she could have more. She *wanted* more.

"John," she said, her voice hoarse.

John had been watching beside them, filming with Max's phone. At his name, he startled.

"Come on over here. Let's make this foursome official."

Max groaned behind her. AJ whispered a strained, "Fuck me, that's hot."

John sidled up beside them. She reached out, wrapping her hand around John's cock, and gave it a pump. He was hard. Ready. Her heart quivered. Was she really going to do this?

Wrapping her lips around John's cock, the debauchery was complete. Three hard cocks in three welcoming holes. *Airtight,* some rational part of her brain seemed to report. The rest was lost in orgasm.

And those orgasms rolled, mini-quakes that kept her body drowned in rapture. Max pushed into her ass. AJ pulled out of her pussy. She caved her cheeks around John's cock. AJ thrust up. Max exited. She released John. Again and again, as sure as the tides rise and fall, until she was nothing but driftwood at the whims of the world.

"You close?" Max asked. At first, she thought the question was for her. She would have laughed hysterically if she had any control left.

AJ replied instead, his voice tight. "Close...Yeah."

"Same," John breathed.

"Me too. Together?"

"'Kay."

As if they'd done this before, their cadence shifted. The steady rhythm became more chaotic. All at once, it wasn't one cock in, the other out—it was both cocks out, both cocks in. In. So far in...

Katie lost herself in a blinding flash of white. They did it again. White. White. A wash of white and nothing but white. And roaring in her ears. And heat flooding her pussy. Her ass. They were coming. Filling her. Emptying their balls into her pussy, her ass, her mouth.

That roaring was her cries. Her screams. Her demands for *more* and *harder* and *fucking come inside of me!*

When it was over—ages and ages later—Katie couldn't move. Like a half-drowned castaway sprawled out on a foreign beach, she was happy to be able to breath. Happy to be alive.

Her lovers seemed to be in a similar state of fatigue. Max pulled free of her ass, but slumped at the end of the bed. AJ appeared passed out beneath her, his softening cock still half-buried in her pussy. It was only when she felt him kiss her neck that she realized he was conscious.

She spent her minutes crawling back to sanity, taking long, steadying breaths. The *pranayama* breathing techniques were back, and with them, a sense of self. She was a very satisfied self.

"Wow," Katie said to no one in particular. She felt as sore and as exhausted as she'd ever felt in her life—and the fatigue wasn't just a physical one. She'd just fucked three guys at once...and loved it.

****

AJ and John left during the early parts of the morning. Katie felt them slide out of bed, but was too exhausted to even say goodbye. When she woke up hours later, she was in Max's arms.

"Morning," she said, sleep in her voice.

"Morning." He sounded like he'd been awake for hours. "Sleep well?"

"You know, I had the craziest dream," she said.

Max laughed. Katie joined him.

finis

ACKNOWLEDGEMENTS

Sequels are hard to write. Unlike an original book, sequels require a steadfast dedication to continuity. Do the characters behave in a consistent way from book to book? Are all the little details that brought them to life captured in the follow-up? Do the plot elements in the new book make sense in the aftermath of the first? Adding to the complexity of a sequel are reader expectations. People have different reading experiences, even if the words are the same, and when we imagine what comes next for the characters, everyone has their own opinions. And after all of those considerations, you still need to write a compelling plot that can stand on its own.

So why did I write *Nothing Forbidden?* Because despite all the challenges, these two characters had more story to tell. Is their story now complete? Is anyone's ever?

The other major reason is that my next saga, *Training to Love It*, prominently features AJ and how he comes into the life of a brand new set of characters. Stay tuned on my site (kennywriter.com), Twitter, and Facebook for news on that one.

So let's get on to the acknowledgements, because I've got a couple major ones to recognize. I'm going to start with my beta readers first because they were instrumental in helping me shape the book as you have it now.

A big thanks to Scott. Remember the challenge of "steadfast dedication to continuity" that I mentioned above? Scott helped make that happen. By now, I'm sure he's sick of reading (and re-reading) these two *Forbidden* titles, but I have to say the outcome has totally been worth it.

I reached out to my other beta reader, Stephen, to authenticate the accounting details for me. He ended up giving some candid advice on the shape of the plot as a whole that not only made it more realistic, but more cohesive.

Both of these readers did exactly what beta readers should do: they were unafraid of constructive criticism. I didn't always follow their advice, but where I did, I couldn't be happier about. Thanks guys!

My editor, the talented Ms. Lucy V. Morgan not only helped make sure my I's were dotted and T's crossed (actually, Google Docs did that, but you get the idea), but she also gave me a female perspective that's critical whenever a male author attempts to write from a woman's point of view.

My wife has begun to take on greater and greater roles in this business, acting as my final set of eyes on both grammar and plot. She's also my partner in life and never ceases to amaze me.

Finally, just as I always do, I have to thank all of you reading this. I have some great fans and more support than I'd ever dreamed. You guys rock.

Until next time!

ABOUT THE AUTHOR

I'm just a guy who writes what I like to read: steamy, explicit erotica that's just crazy enough to be true. I write romantic erotica. I write about characters that I like, and endings that feel natural. I write stories where husbands watch their wives get naughty. I write about MILFs and erotic games and loss of innocence. I believe in a world where men read and appreciate erotica, and hope to contribute to it word by word.

Find me online at www.kennywriter.com, or follow me on Twitter at @kennywriter.

ALSO BY KENNY WRIGHT

After School Special (A Short)

All In: Strip Poker Done Right

Because He's Watching; Ian's Obsession

Cool With Her

Eight Hundred Dollar Heels (A Short)

Just Watch Me

Leap

Moving Mrs. Mitchell (A Short)

Naughty But Nice (A Short)

Rediscovering Danielle (A Short)

Something Forbidden

Unconventional: Business or Pleasure

Wife Watching Shorts, Vol. 1

While She Watches

For a full list of titles, along with their covers, synopses, and where to purchase, go to www.kennywriter.com/books.

18478395R00120

Made in the USA
Middletown, DE
09 March 2015